ERIC & IAN
get a life

Rod Maclean is married with three children,
two dogs, four cats and a mortgage. He lives in
Adelaide and works as a TV news producer.

ERIC & IAN
get a life

ROD MACLEAN

Wakefield Press

Promotion of this book was assisted by the
South Australian government through
Arts South Australia.

Publication of this book was assisted by the
Commonwealth Government through the
Australia Council, its arts funding and advisory body.

Wakefield Press
Box 2266
Kent Town
South Australia 5071

First published 1998

Edited by Fiona Oates
Designed and typeset by Clinton Ellicott, MoBros, Adelaide
Printed and bound by Hyde Park Press, Adelaide

National Library of Australia
Cataloguing-in-publication entry

Maclean, Rod, 1955–   .
Eric and Ian get a life.

ISBN 1 86254 379 8.

I. Title.

A823.3

This book is for Teddi, Wyeth, Myra and Sylvie,
with love and thanks for their help and faith

It was 1966, and Eric and I had both just turned eleven. The two of us had spent the past few years as firm friends at Griffith Primary School. But this year Eric's family had moved to Port Moresby, and he had been left in Canberra to eke out a solo existence in the austere corridors and dormitories of one of the local boarding schools. I thought of innocents murdered at midnight every time I cycled past it.

On weekends, if he wasn't doing detention for his regular misdemeanours, Eric would cut across the hockey fields at Flinders Park, up La Perouse Street, down Caley Crescent, past his family's old house on Wild Street, to Captain Cook Crescent and my place.

We'd pinch some of Dad's filterless Pall Malls and smoke ourselves blue up on Rocky Knob. Or we'd head for the Manuka pool and soggily masticate hot chips drenched with vinegar while marvelling at the sensational mysteries of teenagers clad only in their cozzies kissing beneath the trees. We made suggestive jokes and listened to Eric's trannie with the Beatles singing 'Love, love me do'.

Sometimes we'd go hiking behind Red Hill, hoping we wouldn't be shot in the arse by a territorial farmer who reputedly loaded his shotgun with saltpetre. On one outing – a search for kangaroo skulls and tailbones for our child-primate necklaces – we tossed rocks at a bloated sheep carcass we found near the quarry. Its belly exploded with a blast of putrefaction. The stink swept nausea clean through the pair of us; we lurched away, gasping and giggling at the gruesome sight of all those maggots.

Apart from the time we hid in the birch tree out the front and cracked Mr McCord's windscreen with a hurtling gob of chewy as he motored past, our adventures were harmless and happy. I didn't have anywhere near as much fun when Eric flew up to Port Moresby for holidays and I was left with the likes of Drury Carlton.

I never liked Drury. He bullied people. His idea of fun was army-style marches behind Black Mountain while hauling a sixty-ton pack, numerous blisters, sticky blowflies and six-inch burrs in your socks. He'd call you piss-weak if you wavered. He also stole stuff. I'd complain half-heartedly, afraid of getting caught. But I always shared the booty and certainly made no fuss the time he nicked a copy of *Dare* from the newsagency at Kingston and I got my first stiffy.

The weekend before school resumed, Eric would turn up again with a pocket full of spending money that was meant to last all term. He'd tell me stories from New Guinea on our way down to the Griffith shops for Sunny Boys and twenty cents worth of mixed lollies.

'In Moresby, there are old aerodromes all around the town and wrecked planes and rusty rifles and all sorts of relics.'

He had told me this before. 'So?'

'So, I found a hand grenade.'

I played the expected role. 'Jeez! What'd you do?'

'I thought it was dead, but I pulled the pin and chucked it into a swamp to see if it would explode and it did! There was jungle slime flying everywhere.'

I could picture it clearly. My mental images of warfare were frequently fuelled by visits to the Australian War Memorial Museum and readings from *Battle Picture Library*. The jungle slime spattered at my feet.

'Jeez,' I said again. 'Wow!' This time my awe was real.

'Reckon you could come too, next holidays?'

Naturally, I'd made this request before and been fobbed off with the usual excuses about money and the maybe-next-times that parents invariably use to frustrate a child's impractical ambitions. But this year my lobbying paid off. I was told I could go, but only if I never again attempted to maim my younger brother, Don, with a rabbit chop, and if I absolutely never again told my little sister, Amy, that there was something wrong with her because she didn't have breasts like Barbie.

We flew to Sydney aboard a prop-jet Viscount, drinking free Fanta and souveniring everything from the little cakes of soap in the dunnies to the brown paper sick bags. From Sydney to Brisbane and on up through Cairns to Port Moresby we were in a sleek ultra-modern 727. We demolished our lunches, pinched the stainless-steel knives and forks, and saved the Jatz and cheese, only to find the crackers crushed to powder days later.

Eric's house in Moresby was airy and modern. It was in a brand new subdivision that had been built for people who worked at the university and other Australian colonial benedictions to the Papuan Territory.

We did not spend much time in the house. As soon as

we had dressed and breakfasted, Eric would say, 'Come on, let's explore.'

And Eric's mum would warn us, 'No hitch hiking.'

Eric would dutifully promise, 'No, Mum,' which really meant, 'How else are we going to get into town?'

We went to the markets where women with betel-stained red teeth yelled and laughed and offered us coconuts and strange herbs that were undoubtedly used for shrinking heads. There were Chinese traders with salty plums and hideous fungi in little balsa boxes.

One time, a bloke in a brand new MGB gave us a ride to the movies. The film was being shown in an open-air theatre with deckchairs, and a million mozzies blew in like a squadron of sons of Nippon attacking the Port Moresby beach front at the sinking of the tropical sun. We got in trouble for coming home so late.

Another night, Eric's dad, a botanist, gave a slide show at the university. The pictures were mainly orchids and other species of flowers. I was on the verge of falling asleep when he slipped in a shot of a naked island girl and everyone laughed.

'He always does that,' said Eric, unimpressed. But I was. My parents wouldn't dream of doing such a prank.

Soon after that evening Eric's parents took us to a party at the house next door. The adults were guzzling grog and having a noisy time, with riotous laughter and jazz on the record player. Soon they were pissed.

'Watch this,' said Eric.

He went round offering a tray of food and was politely thanked. Nobody noticed that he was collecting half-empty bottles of beer. Motioning for me to follow, he ferried the bottles to the shadows in the back yard where we downed the tepid brew.

We'd been spotted, though. The two girls of the house had seen what he was up to and pretended to be outraged.

Eric was unperturbed. 'Want some?'

They giggled. 'Better not.'

'Go on.' urged Eric. 'Do you good!'

So the four of us got tipsy and played spin the bottle on the lawn. The girls refused to take off any clothes, but Eric won a kiss. The boy had bravado, that's for sure. Unlike me.

I was having a good holiday. I couldn't wait to go hiking on the Kokoda Trail with Eric and his dad.

At first the going wasn't tough. The path was wide and level. Eric sauntered airily along as if it was just another expedition catching carp down at the Kingston boat harbour. It was clear and not as humid as Moresby. The rustling sea of kunai grass made it impossible for me to see the approaching jungle.

Even when we entered the dark world of the rainforest, it was fascinating rather than frightening. Towering forest trees stood buttressed by gothic roots twenty-feet high, their lower branches festooned with lantana. The air was rank with the woody smell of dark decay. The streams were fresh and clear. We drank often and splashed our faces to cool the sweat.

We came to a village of thatched huts on wooden stilts set in a level clearing. There was no one in sight. A skinny dog barked at us. We ate sandwiches and pressed on in high spirits.

Then the trail started getting steep and muddy. Time after time I'd slip and be fouled by black muck. We'd climb one ridge, me scrambling on hands and knees because my sand-shoes couldn't grip in the mud, only to be confronted by another jungle-wreathed mountain top. We would reach the next apex after a flailing descent and a near drenching in the torrent at the valley base.

This was bearable until the sky above the jungle canopy clouded over and let loose a relentless battering downpour. Eric and I were slipping and swearing. Mr Masters sang the song about Hitler having only one brass ball as he marched us ever onwards.

We scrambled and slithered until at last, having fallen half-way down a slope it had taken me agonising minutes to ascend, I refused to get up.

'Come on, Ian. Dad'll turn us round soon.'

'Then I'll wait for you.'

'Don't give up now!'

'I'm not going any further, Eric. I can't!'

Mr Masters had seen what was going on and he was not impressed. He lectured me about what the Diggers had endured. *They* never admitted defeat ... But he turned us about and led us homewards, cocooned in a contemptuous silence.

I was bringing up the rear when my head and shoulders brushed the leaves of a low-hanging branch. A moment later my body erupted in a dozen fierce explosions of pain. I screamed and flailed about.

'They're inside my shirt!'

'Soldier ants!' yelled Eric as he and his dad came running. Mr Masters slapped with his hat, Eric ripped at my shirt, and the demons were swept away.

When the drama had subsided I heard Mr Masters mumble, 'Serves you right.'

The pain of the bites was nothing compared to the red flare of my shame.

I was beginning to think Eric had been bullshitting about the war relics that he'd claimed were everywhere in Moresby.

We'd been out to the seven-mile drome and explored the earthworks where the Yanks had parked their bombers to protect them from Japanese air raids. The airstrip was mottled with twenty years of regrowth. There was a dump of old fuel drums and rusted wing-tanks that looked as if they belonged on a Mustang. But these were no good to me. I wanted stuff to take home and show off in Canberra.

We climbed Tua Guba, the big hill that overlooked Port Moresby harbour. This was where my father had taken his place among the Australian gunners who manned the mountain-top with their range-finders, Bofors and Ack-Ack guns. They had claimed forty-two Japanese aircraft. One airman had fallen chute-less from his stricken plane clean through the roof of a hospital and survived. Dad had nearly been killed by an American fighter chasing a Zero. I speculated about where the bullets might have ripped the hillside. We combed the bunkers and trenches but didn't find a thing.

Eric shut me up by handing over one of his previous

7

finds, a US Marines battle helmet. The webbing had rotted away and there was a jagged rust-hole right at the crown that made the helmet impossible to wear. But I still thought it was terrific.

And it must have been a good omen, because after that we started finding things everywhere we went.

I kicked a live .45 pistol bullet from an overgrown midden beside a road near the university. We scratched about and found a whole clip of .303 ammo and the rusted block and barrel of a Lee Enfield rifle.

Next we found some machine-gun rounds, probably meant for the weaponry in American aircraft. I imagined the tail gunner in his B-17 with his thumb jammed on the firing pin, shooting out a continuous stream of lethal lead in an attempt to hit one of the Zeros that were spitting out venom as deadly as his own. Did he make it, this hero? Or did they drag him slumped from his cockpit, the rest of the crew wide-eyed at the terror of their own escape?

We knew we should be handing these discoveries over to the army or someone who could dispose of them properly. But instead we hid everything under the house. When the time came to fly home, we wrapped the contraband in clothes and socks: two kids with two suitcases full of unstable, decades-old ammunition.

I was terrified. Not because we could have blown the plane to pieces – I didn't even think of that until later – but of the customs search. I was so nervous I could barely speak.

'Don't act scared,' said Eric, quite calm himself. And then, a touch maliciously, 'They're trained to spot people looking nervous.'

In the Brisbane customs hall, we waited as the line drew closer to the big behemoth of a bloke who was diligently rummaging through every bag. I was about to shit my pants.

It was our turn next. Just as we plonked our bags up for inspection, a flood of tourists from another flight poured into the hall.

'Have a good holiday, son?'

I nodded.

The man looked up at the approaching hordes. He patted our bags. 'Off you go, then.'

I fled.

I took the relics to school for show-and-tell. The teacher went berserk. She ran from the room and returned with the headmaster who quickly impounded everything except the shell casings and the helmet. He called in some bomb disposal expert from Duntroon and my prized possessions were gone.

The biggest shell casing became a home for my pens and pencils. The helmet rusted completely and fell apart.

1966 was a momentous year in Australian history. The first Australian conscript soldiers were sent to Vietnam; the first were killed. Someone tried to assassinate Opposition Leader Arthur Calwell as he left an anti-war rally. The prime minister was happy to say 'All the way with LBJ' as if he was the poor brave bastard about to embark on a troop ship at

Garden Island only to be brought home in a body bag after the battle of Long Tan.

The whole country was in an uproar of controversy and change. 1967 was the same. Prime Minister Harold Holt increased the troop numbers to more than 8000. Gough Whitlam replaced Arthur Calwell as leader of the Labor opposition. In December, Holt disappeared while swimming at Portsea.

But I don't remember any of this. You might say, well, Ian, you were just a kid. You can't be expected to remember everything. Yet as if it was yesterday I can recall Dad erupting from the front door of the house years before in 1963 on the day that President Kennedy died. I had been out on the footpath. My classmate Rosemary Wilson, who lived a few doors down, had been telling me how she had to go to the doctor to find out why she farted so much.

And there's so much else that is clear, before the void: Dad returning from an interstate trip with presents for all in his suitcase; the pock-marks on our living-room floor from ladies' high-heeled party shoes; the time when Don accidentally busted the French doors and needed a million stitches at the Canberra Community Hospital; my own sixteen stitches from the time I patted Jonathan Hough's border collie, unaware it was crazed by a tick burrowing into its brain. And I remember the two-inch refracting telescope Eric and I used to observe the craters of the moon; the plume of smoke from autumn leaves and twigs after Dad had finished pruning the crab apple tree and Mum had made the jelly that tasted so good with buttered toast; polishing my boots and hunting for my stick before the

Saturday hockey match at Jerrabomberra Oval while the FJ warmed up outside the house that was home and had been since the day I'd been born.

But the day President Kennedy died, Dad's eyes looked full of inner panic, as if the universe had just shifted onto an axis of doom. He knew things were changing.

I guess it just took me a few more years to sense the shift.

During the summer holidays of 1966/7, about the time Australia was winning the second test in Cape Town, Mum and Dad took Don, Amy and me for a drive.

'Where are we going?' Don wanted to know.

'You'll see when we get there,' said Dad, sounding pleased with himself.

'Give us a clue,' we demanded.

'Garran,' Dad said.

Wow! This would be fun. Mum and Dad had friends called Garran. They had a big house with a pool on Mugga Way. We'd often go there for races in the water with the other kids while the grown-ups sat in the sun and drank martinis.

'But we haven't got our togs!'

'I meant Garran, the suburb.'

The suburb! What suburb? Garran was in the sticks. It was on the other side of Red Hill in a wilderness of building sites known as Woden Valley.

We motored through Deakin and Hughes to Robson Street and into a cul de sac called Jose Place.

'There it is,' Dad said. 'Number four.'

He pulled up in front of a partly built structure that I could tell was going to be a house. The framework was made of pinus radiata and aluminium-sided sliding windows. There were mounds of sand, cement mixers, bessa bricks left over from the basework, and piles of plastic-wrapped roof tiles.

'We've bought the place!' Dad announced. 'What d'you think?'

There was a clamour of excited approval from Amy and Don. They cascaded out of the car for a closer look, Dad following proudly behind to make sure they didn't fall through the half-finished floorboards.

I refused to leave the car.

'What's the matter, Ian?'

'I hate it!'

Mum tried to mollify me. 'But you'll be able to finish school at Griffith. Your dad and I have already thought of that.'

'I don't care. I still hate it.'

She was genuinely puzzled. 'Why?'

'It's too far for Eric to walk.'

I can't remember my twelfth birthday, but I can remember the fights.

I would pretend they weren't happening, head beneath my pillow and singing to myself to muffle the outraged voices rumbling up the corridor from the living room.

But one night the shouting got so loud I couldn't ignore it. I crept across to Don's room. Amy was already there, both of them in tears. A savage anger rose up inside me and I stormed into the living room where Dad was pointing his accusing finger and yelling at Mum.

'You bastard!' I screamed. Only now do I remember calling him that. 'Leave her alone!'

My father turned to me, shamed but still eaten by his fury. 'I'm not the bastard. She started this.'

What exactly she had started I wasn't told, but the shouting stopped.

Next morning, a dreadful silence filled the kitchen, the frost as palpable as snow on the far Brindabellas. But there were brittle smiles for us kids, as if Mum and Dad were trying to hide what was happening.

I refused to confront what I saw.

Our new house was too far away for Eric to walk to.

But he managed to come for a sleep-over one weekend. We walked up to the shops at the top of Robson Street and bought some dried peas to put in the ends of the Bic pens we'd fashioned as pea-shooters. We were planning a war in the trenches of the building sites that zig-zagged up and down the slopes of Garran.

Eric got me in the eye with a pea. It hurt like buggery so I petulantly tossed back a clod of dirt. It hit him smack in the back of the head, exploding like a star shell.

'Bastard!' he yelled. 'You did that on purpose.'

My eye was still screwed up in pain. He must have thought my face was as mad as his so he took a swing at me and soon we were wrestling in the muddy bottom of a trench, limbs writhing as both of us sought to get a decent stranglehold.

'Give up?'

Grunts and swearing.

'Give?'

'Go to hell!'

Eventually my strength wore down and Eric had an arm around my throat and another gripping my wrist so it felt about to break.

'Give!'

I subsided.

He let go and we looked at each other with gladiatorial respect, part heart-thumping pride, part breathless stupidity. It was only when he'd stopped trying to clean the dirt off his clothes that I realised there were tears in his eyes. I was shocked. Eric never cried.

'You all right?'

He nodded dumbly.

'Shit. You won, Eric.'

Still he said nothing. He climbed out of the trench and started walking towards Jose Place. I followed him, anxious that I'd displeased my friend.

'What's the matter?'

'My parents are coming home.'

I didn't understand. That was supposed to be good news. It meant he'd be able to leave the boarding school, maybe we'd even be reunited for our final year of primary school, back together at Griffith where our mateship began.

'But that's good, isn't it?'

'No, it bloody isn't!' And he was crying again. 'They're

getting divorced. Dad's going to Kenya. And I have to stay at the Grammar school . . .'

I wonder now if Eric also has a selective memory about what happened after his world shifted onto the axis of doom. At that stage, mine was still turning.

At the start of 1968 my family moved back to Captain Cook Crescent and I was enrolled at Narrabundah High School.

Dad explained the move as an economic decision, claiming he had not been able to sell the old house because everyone was moving to Canberra's newer suburbs and there was no market for the older ones.

But now I piece it all together again, I see there must have been another reason.

One afternoon, Dad called the three of us kids into the living room where Mum was waiting too. She had an awkward look, big filmy eyes that looked as if they needed to shield us from the hurt we were about to endure. Dad did the talking.

'Your mum and I are getting a divorce.'

Silence.

'I've been offered a new job in Thailand, with an organisation called SEATO. I'll be taking it up in a month or so. And guess what?'

He hoped, I suppose, to make something positive out of the mess.

'I told them I'd only take the job if you three can come and visit me. Every Christmas holiday. They said yes.'

It worked for a while. The promise of adventure must have been more powerful than the impossibility of considering life without both of our parents.

But later when I passed Amy in the corridor I could tell she'd been crying. And a day or so later, Don was sitting outside on the roof of the garden shed, arms wrapped around his knees, refusing to come down.

'What's up with you?'

For a moment he said nothing. Then it blurted out. 'Mum's got a new boyfriend. Dad told me. They're getting married.'

'What!'

'His name's Paul. And get this. He has daughters. Nadine and Carole. And guess what else?'

'What?'

'We're moving again.'

I kicked the side of the shed. I found myself out on Captain Cook Crescent, running. Anywhere. I didn't care. Anywhere.

No, not anywhere.

To Eric's. To the one true friend I had in a world that was steadily robbing me of all the secure stability I thought was my due.

In 1969, the fog of confusion that shrouded our world lifted long enough for Eric and me to wag school and watch together in awe as astronaut Armstrong planted a dusty boot on the moon.

Then the mists rolled back in, and with the fog came that rampant, randy stage in life when the hormones rule the brain.

Angela and Veronica Maxwell were the stunning statuesque twins who lived next door after we moved, minus Dad and in the company of step-father Paul and step-sisters Nadine and Carole, across Lake Burley Griffin, and even further from Eric, to Ainslie.

The twins always looked down their perfect noses at me and Don as if they were examining a collection of sheep dags. We forgave them this snobbery because, as Eric correctly observed when I told him about our sexy new neighbours, being barely into your teens is no great attraction for girls in their matriculation year. What's more they went to Watson – McDonald High School's traditional foe. Don and I weren't just juvenile dags, we were enemy juvenile dags.

Eric was in second form at the Grammar School and could only visit on weekends. He stood no chance with the Maxwell girls either, as he was tarnished by his association with me and Don and Don's new schoolmate Collum. Collum always whistled loudly and lewdly whenever he saw the twins pass by, breasty and bursting at their Watson-blue blouses.

Despite his realism about our chances with the Maxwells, as soon as Eric saw these gorgeous girls for himself, he lamented, 'It's not fair!'

Which meant that he was going to hatch a scheme to rectify the injustice. And he did.

I'd borrowed Peter Weston's air rifle and bought a packet

of slugs, so Eric and I decided to do some target practice on the slopes of Mount Ainslie, above Duffy Street. This was a favourite adventure ground of ours, a convenient place to escape the burdensome attention of parents. The bush began as soon as the houses stopped. We would scavenge in the Hackett tip or head towards the storm drains near Antill Street to look for people's cracker-night bonfires to torch. Or we could go the other way and look down on the migrant hostel, the war memorial, and, if the season was right, the squads of footballers or Cordies from Duntroon being badgered along Mount Ainslie Drive by coaches megaphoning from the comfort of their cars.

This particular day we wandered up towards the big watertank to see if anyone had left a girlie magazine stashed in the bushes. No luck there, so we shared a cigarette we'd pinched from Collum's place, set up some dented Coke cans, and started shooting.

I was on a good round when Eric suggested his plan. I missed the last shot.

'And how do you reckon we'll do that without getting sprung?'

'Easy! We pretend to be doing something else, and make the hole while no one's looking.'

'Like what are we s'posed to be doing?'

'We'll make a target.'

Eric took the slug gun and fired off a shot that just missed a passing rosella. It squawked at us as Eric led the way downhill with lust in his eyes.

The Maxwell twins' bedroom faced the side of our house that featured a frequently populated balcony and a just as frequently used driveway. So, despite the apparently innocent clutter of wood and tools and some useful bushes, doing the job undetected wasn't easy. But at last Eric managed to drill a couple of half-inch holes through the fence.

We had clear line of sight!

The wait for dark was agonising. We splurged forty cents on a packet of Marlboros and loitered in the Wakefield Gardens, fantasising.

'What do you reckon they'll look like?'

'Big! You reckon we'll see?'

'Brown nipples?'

'Pink.'

'Maybe they're lesbians!'

Back home, I barely tasted dinner, continually turning to survey the depth of twilight through the windows behind me.

We astonished everyone by volunteering to do the washing up. Then we declared that we were going to play chess in my room. We started a game to see if anyone cared about our whereabouts. As usual, they didn't.

Just before nine o'clock we climbed out my bedroom window and took up our positions at the fence.

The lights were on, the curtains were open. We could even hear voices. There was movement in a corner of their room. Then Angela appeared right in front of the window. She was fiddling with the buttons of a silky blouse.

Eric groaned in the darkness.

But Angela was buttoning up. It was my turn to groan.

'They're going out!'

The girls were fussing with scents and earrings and pouting in a big mirror. A few minutes later we heard a car pull up with a polite toot. The twins took up their handbags and the room went dark. We scurried to the top of the driveway in time to see Angela and Veronica being ushered into a gleaming 1964 Ford Mustang by none other than Dan 'Dimwit' Johnstone, a Watson prefect and captain of their dreaded rugby team. Eric chucked a rock at the departing car. It bounced off the boot. The brake lights came on and Johnstone climbed out to see what had happened. By which time, of course, we were well hidden.

Back in my room, the Saturday night hits were droning away and the chess game was undisturbed. Resigned to a long wait, we finished the game. We were set to play another but Eric advanced a few pieces into impossible territory, realised what he'd done, and tipped the board over.

'Let's get out of here.'

We ranged about for ages. It was well after midnight when we took up positions in a tree in the park across from the Maxwells'. Eric fished out more Marlboros and we settled in for the wait.

The girls came home at about half-past one. This time the Mustang took off with a raucous blast of the horn and the girls responded with tipsy waves and laughter. Eric grinned in the darkness. We shinned down the tree and hurried to our spy holes.

They were already occupied. By Don and Collum.

Eric hissed, 'Piss off, you two!'

'We were here first.'

The lights went on in the twins' room. Eric had a look of urgent desperation.

'We made the bloody holes. Piss *off*!'

Eric tried to haul Collum away from his hole, which was a bad mistake because Collum had grown up in Italy and had an arsenal of techniques he'd later employ as a hooker in the school's senior scrum.

Eric got a knee in the nuts. He grunted an oath and lurched against one of the bushes lining the fence. This set off a loud clatter of leaves and limbs.

Suddenly the window flew open next door; we didn't have time to duck. The Maxwell girls were peering through the gloom, straight at us.

Veronica was seething like a boiler about to blow a bolt.

'You filthy animals!'

Angela hissed something about vermin and swished the curtains shut.

I rounded on Don. 'You stupid bastards, look what you've done now.'

'You're the stupid bastards. When you were drilling your bloody holes this arvo, if you had any brains, you would've seen a few there already.'

Collum laughed.

Eric and I just looked at each other, then at the fence, then at the curtains now eternally drawn.

It's not easy to look dignified when you've just copped a knee in the nads, but Eric dusted himself off, drew himself to his full height and, with his best withering glare, delivered his judgment.

'What a pair of perverts.'

When Goldsmith strangled the chicken, our disgust with Don and Collum only intensified.

Goldsmith was Don and Collum's mate, a big, good-looking, raw-boned blond idiot. He had a first name but everyone called him Goldsmith.

The three of them decided they would go camping at the Cotter reserve and, just to shit them off, Eric and I said we would go too.

In those days the Cotter was a great place for adventures. There was a flying fox roped across a big pool that was dammed up by a low weir. Dragonflies fizzed about and trout lay in the higher pools where the sedge flies hatched. A fallen log bridged the upper stream and crossed to a track that led to the caves. On the hills a tangle of blackberries held the delicious promise of making your fingers sticky-purple with juice. And all the while there was the hair-raising suspicion of snakes.

No one knew much about camping but eventually the five of us managed to erect Collum's dad's ex-army tent. This jungle-green colossus was so heavy it took two of us just to roll it out, and so muggy inside we could hardly breathe until someone observed that it might be smart to open the flaps.

We then agreed that we had to collect firewood. Goldsmith, Don and Collum headed off into the wilderness, and naturally Eric and I went the other way. We headed towards the dam, past the kiosk and the picnic grounds, over the swing bridge that jounced up and down as we crossed high above the rocks and the babble of the river, and ascended alongside the cliffs to the towering concrete face of the Cotter dam. Here we could view the smooth-water serenity of the reservoir against the majestic back-ground of black-green pine forest and the distance-hazed ranges.

We were surveying the scenery in appreciative silence when we heard giggling. Three girls were climbing the hundreds of concrete steps towards us.

Eric wasn't the best-looking bloke in the world, but there was a certain charm in his crooked grin and a come-with-me-and-taste-forbidden-fruit invitation in his dark eyes. He swaggered forward to meet the girls.

'G'day. I'm Eric. This is Ian.'

The girls examined us doubtfully. One of them started to turn away. But the tallest – a redhead with freckles and frank green eyes – announced that her name was Sheena.

Sheena nudged a small blonde whose arms and legs glowed with a honey-coloured tan.

'This is Pru.' Pru giggled. There was a pause. 'And this is Amanda.'

Dark-haired and disapproving, Amanda had been the one set to turn away. Now she completed the manoeuvre. That didn't bother Eric. He'd sized up the situation – all this time Sheena had been looking at me – and was latching on to Pru while I pretended to be nonchalant, leaning against the railing that prevented people from tumbling over the dam's downstream precipice wall.

Sheena came and stood beside me. She was wearing a strong sweet perfume.

'It's pretty here.'

It certainly was, and I agreed with her. 'Do you come here often?'

'No, this is the first time. We're from Melbourne.'

'On holidays?'

'Camping. All our families. Caravans all drawn up together like a wagon train.'

We'd seen them on our walk to the dam. 'Like you're about to be attacked by Red Indians.'

'That's them.'

'That's not far from our tent.' I gathered my courage and ventured the suggestion, 'We could show you round.'

Sheena gave me a smile that stirred me up. I was confused by the thumping in my heart.

'Okay. But we're expected back soon. Tomorrow?'

I nodded immediately, dumbstruck that my suggestion had actually succeeded. She gave me a conspiratorial smile. I managed to return it.

When we got back to the tent, the others were missing. We pinched some firewood from unattended campsites and built a blaze. Then we took a couple of Goldsmith's tailor-mades and smoked in the gathering darkness. Eric lay on his back looking up at the evening star and, as he often did, started talking about life beyond the planet.

'It doesn't make sense that we're the only life in all that huge space. So life must be out there somewhere. Mustn't it?'

'You read too much science fiction.'

'At least I *can* read. Anyway, what's on your mind? As if I didn't know.'

I chucked a pebble at him. He let it hit and laughed.

'You know what I'd do if I were you?'

'What?'

'Skip first base and try to get a feel of Sheena's tits.'

'I'll give her a kiss *and* have a feel.'

We discussed the possibilities of this fabulous topic for long lascivious minutes and were just turning our thoughts to dinner when the problem was solved for us.

Don and Collum came running up ahead of Goldsmith, who was stumbling along with something lumpy in the bag that normally held the tent-poles. All three were looking anxiously about to make sure no one was watching or following.

Satisfied that they were safe, Goldsmith emptied the bag.

Out came a chicken, a big white layer hen with a red comb. It flopped to the ground with a dead-eyed angry glare.

'Jesus, that was close!'

'We got into the keeper's yard . . .'

'. . . Goldsmith gets hold of the chicken and he strangles it!'

'Except the bloody thing starts struggling and lets out this terrible squawk and feathers are flying everywhere!'

'And the dog starts barking and someone's at the back door . . .'

The three were still gasping for air and looking crazed with panic and excitement.

'So I just smashed its head against a fencepost!'

'And we ran like buggery . . .'

They ran out of words and just stood there, appraising their victim. Finally Goldsmith lit a smoke, took a heaving drag and inquired, with the genuine curiosity of the stupid, 'How d'you cook it?'

Eric laughed. 'In New Guinea they boil 'em and pluck 'em, then chop 'em up for a barbecue in the ashes.'

'They do that everywhere, stupid.' This was Collum on his high horse of perpetual smart-arsedom. 'But where's the pot?'

Eric was unruffled. 'Lacking a pot, Collum, you'll have to chuck it in the fire to burn the feathers off, then let the fire burn down and cook the chook in the coals.'

Everyone argued about this until Goldsmith concluded that Eric's was the only way he could think of that had a chance of working. In any case, his hunger was more important than slighting Collum by siding with Eric.

Goldsmith tossed the bird into the flames. The feathers caught immediately, fuelling the creature's pyre. I could see the trio's faces in the firelight. They looked a little appalled at the consequences of their murder.

The chicken took ages to cook, and it was still so under-done we had to use Eric's fishing knife to carve it bone from bone to get a share. Eric gnawed his bit of leg and thigh with gusto and demanded more. All I could taste was dirt and woodsmoke and slimy meat. Conscience forgotten, the others bragged about their exploits and ate like grimy warriors, their grease-smeared faces streaked by charcoal.

When Eric told them of our own adventures that afternoon, they scoffed and howled and declared we were bullshit artists.

They realised the truth of our claims next morning when Sheena and Pru came sauntering past the tent to see if Eric and I were home.

Eric grinned. 'Beauty! No Amanda.'

Goldsmith and Collum looked at the girls. Then they bounded into the sunlight with brazen greetings, Collum wearing only his Y-fronts and waving himself about.

They didn't stand a chance. We'd been up and dressed for ages. We were out of the tent in seconds, wishing the girls a breezy good morning and proposing a walk to the caves while Goldsmith was still hopping about trying to get his shoes on. Don watched blearily from the tent as Eric gave the three of them a two-finger salute and we started along the path to the caves. Sheena and I led the way.

'Nice friends you've got.'

I was alarmed. Did this mean that Sheena actually liked the look of Goldsmith? Or worse, Collum?

'They're not my friends. They're Don's. My little brother. They're a real pain.'

It was one of those perfectly clear mornings you get during autumn on the southern tablelands and in the lower mountains. Deciduous leaves flared with rusty brilliance after the first few frosty nights. Everything crackled or crunched underfoot. Our breaths steamed with the effort of the climb.

Sheena grabbed my hand so I could help her up a steep part of the track. When it levelled again she left her fingers entwined in mine. Eric wolf-whistled from behind us.

'Shuddup!' I yelled back. But when I went to pull my hand away, embarrassed, Sheena held on.

'It's nice like this.'

She was brushing against me in ways that the width of the track didn't really make necessary.

Most of the Cotter caves were too narrow for anyone except a serious midget. But the biggest boasted a large main cavern and numerous off-shoots that were home to hundreds of bats and human myths and mysteries.

We reached the entrance and waited for Eric and Pru to catch up. Sheena looked into the depths and shuddered.

'I don't like it.'

I gave my manliest chuckle. 'It's okay. There's nothing to be scared of. Except a few bats.'

'I *hate* bats. I'm not going in there.'

'We'll stay away from where they live. I swear.'

She considered the quality of my promise. 'All right. But make sure we do.'

So this was to be the day Eric and I added our names to the legends of the Cotter caves.

We descended the wooden staircase that had been built years before. Sheena was gripping my arm so tightly that the circulation started tingling from starvation.

The light from the cave entrance faded into total darkness. Eric and I telepathically edged towards a place where the cavern floor was free of rocks and sloped only gently. Sheena hung on in genuine terror. When she saw the booming blackness of our intended destination she hauled me back towards the light.

'I'm not going on!'

'Come on, there's nothing to worry about.'

'No! Take me back.'

Eric saved the day. Some inspiration had made him bring along his radio. He raised 2CA, which tuned in with amazing clarity. The sound of Dave Edmunds rang out. 'I hear you knocking, but you can't come in . . .'

Sheena subsided a little and we were able to sit together, facing the entrance so Sheena could see the suggestion of light, and listen to the music. She began to relax.

My arm went around her shoulders as she snuggled in closer and put her face up to mine for a kiss. I gave her a clumsy exploratory peck, but she wasn't stopping with that. I felt the tip of her tongue tickling along the inside of my upper lip. My brain exploded. We kissed again. I reached for the swell of her breasts.

Suddenly I felt a vicious pain just below the elbow of the arm I had around Sheena. I let out a yelp and Sheena sprang yowling away, her screams ricocheting off the cave walls like demons.

Goldsmith. He'd been hiding in the gloom. He flicked on his torch and shone it on his face from under his chin, making a grotesque mask of his stupid grinning features. He was laughing so hard he couldn't talk.

Two more torches came on to reveal Don and Collum dancing about like dervish ghosts.

'Bastards!'

I lunged for Goldsmith, determined to beat the crap out of him, but he blinded me with his torch then turned it off and disappeared.

'You'll die for this, Goldsmith!'

The trio laughed like ghouls.

Sheena and Pru were half-way up the stairs. Eric scrambled to stop them, but he had no hope. I made the entrance just in time to blink at the unexpected sight of Sheena and Pru being confronted by Amanda and a posse of parents.

'We have to go now,' said Sheena.

And the two girls were herded away. Further down the hill, Sheena turned and gave me a wave. I knew I'd be smart to cherish it, because it was all I was getting.

'Bye, girls.' Goldsmith waved from the top of the stairs. The Cotter Caves Chicken Strangler. A big blond fool leering and waving and prancing about like a mountain climber touched by Saint Vitas' Fire.

I looked at my arm. There were teeth marks in the elbow.

I was not adapting well to my new family situation.

Not wanting to blame either Mum or Dad for the collapse of their marriage, it was convenient to lay the guilt on the interloper, my step-father, Paul. I did so silently, never confronting him, but always implying that I would never accept him. I obeyed his commands with bad grace, and churlishly refused to detail my day at school when at the dinner table he asked us one-by-one what we'd learned.

'Nothing.'

'Oh, come now,' he'd say in his English accent, 'you must have learned something.'

'Nope.'

'He's too stupid to learn.' This from Nadine, who was older than me by a year. She was a straight-A student, and fluent in French after her time with Carole at a Swiss boarding school.

Naturally, I'd come in like the tide. 'I'm smarter than you.'

'Oh?' she'd say, her thin eyebrows arching with all the snobbishness of a Maxwell. 'Then perhaps you'll tell me what *cochon* means.'

'Of course I know, but I'm not telling you.'

'What a pity. It describes you to a tee.'

Surprisingly, Nadine's superior attitude had a beneficial effect. I decided I'd show the bitch a thing or two when it came to getting good marks, and, apart from maths, I was doing reasonably well at school.

Eric had no such inspiration. I'd heard him say a hundred times how much he hated his school, and now he was telling his mum. She'd kept him at the Grammar School even after Eric's dad had left for Kenya. She answered his pleas for her to let him attend McDonald with me with, 'Grammar is a good school, Eric.' She reasoned that McDonald was on the north side of Canberra, and they lived on the south. She said that if Eric changed schools, he'd have to go somewhere closer like Telopea Park or Narrabundah.

'Then let me go there. Anywhere! Mum, I can't stand that place!'

For a while, his mum resisted. But by the middle of 1970, Eric had won his way to Telopea Park.

Eric's mum didn't have the advantage of a new boyfriend to help her rebuild her life. But she resurrected her mathematics degree, forgotten while she'd been buried in the role of housewife, retrained in the new world of computing, and before long she had a job teaching at ANU.

In my hybrid house at Ainslie, the only place I had any claim to was my bedroom. At Eric's, we gathered in the lounge room to drink coffee and eat toast and butter with melon jam amid the fascinating clutter of a house dedicated to challenge and learning.

Eric's mum liked classical music, but, unlike Paul, she didn't mind if we played Bob Dylan or the Animals. She had a copy of Germaine Greer's *The Female Eunuch* and discussed its contents with her girls. She passionately congratulated Gough Whitlam for pledging free universities if he won government. She shed tears when she saw the news on television about the killing of anti-war protesters at Kent State University. She wore a Vietnam Moratorium badge and wanted to know what I'd do if the war went on and I was conscripted.

'I dunno.'

'Well, I hope you won't be. But you should think about it. Your fathers fought a war for freedom against tyranny. What's this one about?'

'Beating communism?'

'Ah, the dear old domino theory. Do you know what that is?'

'No.'

'I suggest you find out. Read. Learn. Make your own decisions and choices. So that if you go to Vietnam, you go because you want to.'

Mrs Masters was always saying things like that. She enthused about the election of Australia's first Aboriginal senator. She said she supported the idea of land rights.

'Why?' asked Eric.

'They were here first,' I replied.

'They just want a hand out like they always do. They'll chop up their places for firewood.'

I was about to get angry, but I saw Eric and his mum share an amused glance and I knew they'd set me up.

'Oh, and Eric,' I said, feeling very clever. 'I suppose you'd disagree with Bertram Wainer.'

'About what?'

'That abortion is the lesser of two evils.'

Mrs Masters gave me a look of approval, as if to say, 'You're learning, boy.'

I had a lot of time for Eric's mum. And, though it was no fault of Mum's or Paul's, I felt much more at home at Eric's place than at mine.

In the summer of 1971/2, Eric and I finished negotiating the School Certificate exams. Eric's mum had promised him that if he did well he'd at last be allowed to join me at

McDonald High. But by the time Don, Amy and I hopped on the plane to Thailand, the results weren't in and the white shirt of senior school seemed a long way off.

Going to Bangkok was a real holiday. I was all set to bounce Don off the walls of the squash court at the British Club, or to hang around the reading room with *Candi* in a cane chaise lounge. If we got bored we could do battle with the cues in the snooker room with the big ceiling fans whirring above. I looked forward to shandies and *kao pad* at the open-air bar by the pool; chocolate-covered ice creams and paperbacks beneath the sunshades; and dips in the pool when the heat became too strong.

Maybe Dad would rent the embassy house at Pattaya and we'd hire a fishing boat for the day so we could all compete to see who'd catch the most *pla kapong*. We'd eat crabs picked live from cages on an island in the gulf. We'd go water-skiing after lunch, and maybe fish some more on the lazy run back to Pattaya.

Maybe Don and I would hire Honda 50 stepthroughs and tour the dusty tracks that snaked among the paddies and sago fields between rickety wooden hamlets and villages. We would admire the paintwork on the roofs of the golden *wats* and sample sweet tea drinks in plastic bags with straws from roadside stalls. And Dad would certainly take us to Dolf Rick's famous waterfront restaurant where he'd inevitably order a fruit-of-the-sea casserole while we'd gorge on steak and chips. That was how it had always been.

But this visit was different. By day we saw almost nothing of Dad. There was an important SEATO conference coming up and it seemed to us that Dad was organising the whole event. After hours, Dad was immersed in *The Importance of Being Earnest*, which he was directing for the Bangkok Community Theatre.

Amateur theatrics were my father's true passion. I could remember being dragged to performances of all varieties, from *Love Rides the Rails* to *The Glass Menagerie*. These shows were staged by the Canberra Repertory Theatre, which operated from some war-surplus Nissen huts not far from Kingston and close to the hangars that stored the Australian Archives. The huts were also near the shores of the lake, which had only recently been filled, drowning the fords and the remnants of the old wooden bridge that had once guided traffic along Commonwealth Avenue and across the Molonglo to the dusty northern shore and Civic.

When he wasn't flying off to Perth or Washington, or dressing in his penguin suit for some diplomatic party or another, Dad was either playing pennant tennis at Red Hill, wicket-keeping at Manuka, or involved in a Rep theatre show. In Thailand, he had found an immediate place among the expatriate thespians of Siam.

Dad's apartment on Rama VI Road was always full of theatrical types. We could tell Dad was sweet on one ofthem, an elegant lady named Sally. She was playing Gwendolyn. There was also a suave Englishman named Gavin who was playing Ernest, and he was a definite rival in the Sally stakes.

I developed a crush on a pretty anthropologist named

Christine who talked enthusiastically about the discovery of an ancient rice-growing culture in the hills up north. She promised to take me there one day.

Charles was a flame-bearded New Zealander who ran a girlie bar on Sukhumvit Road. The bar was frequented by American soldiers on leave from Vietnam.

Stan and Marcia were Peace Corps volunteers from Texas. Marcia had a role in the play, Stan was the technical director. His offsider was an American reporter named Sam who claimed to have witnessed the aftermath of some sort of massacre in Vietnam at a place called Mylai.

This sophisticated international cast would turn up at Dad's place with duty-free bottles of Johnny Walker and Smirnoff and exotic beers like Carlsberg, Tuborg and Lowenbrau. Thrilled to be in such company and encouraged to act as they did, Don and I guzzled the beers and smoked Lucky Strikes and Camels. We all helped to coach the actors with their lines, and after the work was done we'd join in the hilarious drunken games of charades. We stayed up for hours, ogling the fun on offer in adulthood.

The Bangkok Company Theatre hired a place called the Villa Club to stage the play. The club was a ramshackle complex owned by an unusually tall Thai who had Brill-creamed hair and promoted performances of Thai classical dancing in the theatre. He profited handsomely by selling Mekong whisky and local beers in the adjacent bar.

Dad put us kids to work. Don designed the publicity posters and painted the portraits adorning the set. Amy worked on costumes and helped sort out the chaos backstage. I spent precarious hours high in the rigging with Sam, setting gelled lights and spots. I had been given the job of monitoring the stage lighting during performances, so one night after rehearsal I stayed back with Sam to learn how the ancient fader board worked.

The lighting room was a cubicle attached to the main building by some dubious scaffolding and a wobbly set of stairs. You could walk out onto the roof and view the low smoggy sprawl of the city. Inside the cubicle there was a slit window so that you could see the stage. There was also a prehistoric intercom to take instructions from the stage manager. I learned the ropes in no time.

But Sam was not in a hurry. 'You ever smoked a reefer?' he asked me.

I'd heard of marijuana, of course. I was growing up in the seventies. 'No.'

'Want to try?'

Sam fished in his shirt pocket and brought out a hand-rolled cigarette, thin but tightly packed. He lit up and dragged hard with a hissing intake of air, stepping out into the night air as he did so.

'Best *boodah*,' he gurgled, still holding his breath to keep in the smoke.

He passed the joint to me and I sucked and coughed. I sucked again, harder, and fought back the urge to splutter.

The effect was almost immediate. My ears were assaulted by intense noise from the ceaseless flow of traffic on Sukhumvit Road. I could smell the belching fumes from buses, taxis and *samlors*. Suddenly the city looked like one of those postcards captured by a time-lapse exposure. Vivid neon advertising signs blared with excitement for Seiko and

Mitsubishi. Enormous floodlit paintings proclaimed the latest Chinese and Indian movies high above the long luminous trails of headlights and tail-lights that flowed to and from this bustling city known as the Venice of the East. All of a sudden I could taste its spices. I could speak its language.

Sam drove me home through the blur of traffic. A powerful tape deck loaded with Hendrix wailed full bore. Foxy Lady. How Ernest felt about Gwendolyn, Dad about Sally. I laughed as I puffed more of the magic weed and Sam cruised through the chaos.

When I got home I stayed up all night doing a drawing of Gwendolyn in Victorian costume being serenaded by a freaked out Ernest in rampaging Afro.

I met an American kid from the International School. He slipped me a reefer when I asked, as casually as I could, if he knew where I could get some. I smoked it on opening night, alone on the roof of the Villa Club. Unfortunately I neglected to raise the stage lights for Scene One and big Texan Stan had to yell at me through the intercom.

After that I managed to concentrate, and gave an inspired performance on the fader board. Dad's direction was highly praised in next morning's *Bangkok Post*, as were Don's set decorations. Alas, the Chopin in the cubicle did not rate a mention.

The show finished its season and we finally got to go to Pattaya. I had a mission: seek and purchase *boodah*.

I set out on a hired Honda stepthrough. A farmer guided me to a thatched hut built on stilts to help it cope with the

Wet Season floods and the irrigation of the paddies. The hut was bare-floored and open-sided from window level up. There were about two dozen dark olive-coloured plants drying on racks. The whole place reeked of resin.

The hut's owner asked me how much I wanted. I told him *nitnoy*, a little bit, and he shrugged and gave me a small package. It cost me *sipsong baht*, a dollar. Nothing! I paid happily then puttered away on my stepthrough, bent on getting stoned.

Stan and Marcia had also come down from Bangkok. Next day we all took a fishing boat over to the islands. The fishing was good – between us we landed near fifty of the beautiful sea-perch that were prized at the Sunday markets.

We beached for lunch. Dad could barely restrain himself in anticipation of freshly cooked crab, so he hopped off the boat with Don and Amy. They made a bee-line for the thatch-shaded restaurant with its tables in the sand.

Stan and Marcia stayed behind and we smoked some of the farmer's grass. I reckon Dad would have smoked some too if I had offered it. When Stan and Marcia went off to eat, I cracked a can of Tuborg and started an intricate sketch of a mangrove root system. I loved the way its roots dug into the perfect white sand. The roots turned to legs and suddenly I was looking at a Chinese cat so I sketched that too, a double-exposed photo where the combined images were as real as the originals.

'Wow,' said Marcia, back for a packet of cigarettes. 'What planet have *you* been on?'

I had no idea. It certainly did not seem like the foggy

world of my childhood. In this new world visions and perceptions presented themselves at every puff.

Our holiday drew to an end. Sam left for Cambodia, and I left for Canberra with his parting gift – a twine-bound stick of marijuana stashed in my socks.

It would blow Eric away.

Eric was bursting with news. His eyes gleamed with pride and pleasure as he fished a piece of paper from his jeans pocket.

'Six A's!'

'You're coming to McDonald!'

He was grinning like an idiot. He'd campaigned so long for this moment and now he had finally succeeded.

I knew exactly how we should celebrate. We headed up the Duffy Street track, away from prying eyes.

We smoked the entire Thai stick between us. Eric was mightily impressed and mightily stoned. His amused, cunning eyes turned red and he settled on his back in the grass with a beatific smile.

'I do declare I'm bloody transmogrified. Shit! Where do we get some more?'

'Jack Winters, King of the Hippies.'

'At McDonald?'

I nodded.

'I knew there was a reason for coming to your crappy school.'

Jack Winters had long blond hair, John Lennon glasses, and a cool easy smile that let you know that he knew what was going down. And that whatever it was, it was definitely okay with him.

The school hierarchy didn't mind when Jack wrote passionate anti-war stories and poems for the school magazine. But there had been trouble over one episode during the Moratorium marches when he had dared to challenge one of the senior maths teachers over his involvement in training military cadets. Jack had copped six cuts of the cane and had gone around showing everyone the welts, saying that corporal punishment was only a small step away from murder.

Jack was a swift long-distance runner, starting guard on the senior basketball team, and captain of Daly House. I was elected to be his deputy.

Our school house was the defending champion of swimming and athletics, and Jack didn't intend to let these titles slip. '1972,' he proclaimed, 'will be the year of Winters in summer.'

The campaign began with the school's swimming carnival. Jack had made up some charismatic war cries and he soon had the 150 students of Daly House united as a raucous, banner-waving cheer squad. I learned the chants and pranced about next to Jack with my long black hair and copycat John Lennon glasses, enthusing with a cardboard megaphone as if I was a slightly taller incarnation of Jack himself.

At one point, a bloated smart-arse from Sixth Form

named Udo Linz came up to me with a malicious smile, sweating and squinting through his grease-smeared glasses.

'I challenge you to think of something original.'

'Piss off, shithead.'

He bellied off, laughing. 'Piss off, shithead! What a comeback!'

He disappeared behind the stands, but I could still hear him guffawing over the din of the races.

I masked my fury by coming fourth in the backstroke, my best result all day. But at least I gave the competition a burst, unlike Linz who loafed with a book under the stands. Screw him, anyway, this was fun and involvement. The power of Jack had caught me. I led the chants when he went to check the scores. We won hands down.

Jack shook my hand. 'Thanks for your support, man.'

'We'll do it again at athletics,' I proclaimed.

He nodded at this certainty. 'Me 'n Ked 'n Franes are goin' to the Rex for a few beers. Wanna come?'

We went in Ked's car, a rattling EH with more holes than an outback road sign. Ked and Franes also had John Lennon glasses and long straight hair, although Ked's hair was a blazing orange red. He had a craggy Celtic face with a big beaked nose and a beard almost as long and thick as his hair. The straights at school thought Ked was nuts because he went around quoting poems and song titles like 'Several Species of Small Furry Animals Gathered Together in a Cave and Grooving with a Pict'.

So there we were lighting up Chesterfields as Ked drove us to the tartaned seclusion of the Scottish bar at the Rex, which was renowned for serving beer to minors. Chesterfields were the new fashion, and Jack offered me one of his. Then he looked at me speculatively and pulled out a joint.

'What about one of these?'

'*Boodah*?'

They relaxed.

'Wish it was,' said Jack, sniffing the joint as if it was a Cuban cigar. 'Queensland heads though. Not bad shit.'

He let me do the honours. As I lit up, I thought, 'You beauty. Eric and I are in!'

I had no way of knowing just how far.

On Friday nights, Eric would dump his schoolbag at my place and we'd hoof it down to the fountain at Garema Place. The fountain was one of Canberra's few gathering places for young people who were interested in trying things that their parents frowned upon.

Jack, Ked and Franes were usually there. So was a drop-out bloke named Eddie, who had wealthy parents, a flash house in Campbell, and his own in-need-of-restoration post-war Norton.

There was also usually a group of kids from Canberra High, who we tolerated even though the school was another of McDonald's sporting enemies.

Most Fridays we would find someone willing to sell us a joint or two. We'd bludge cigarettes and hang about, watching the shoppers flurry by in a tizz, listening to Jack carry on about politics and the war, and helping Ked and Franes argue about whether King Crimson was a better band than Emerson Lake and Palmer.

I met Gwen at the fountain. Eric knew her from his last year at Grammar when the boys had been press-ganged for socials with the CCEGS girls.

Gwen had lovely tight-curled blonde hair, a perfect rosy complexion and a full-lipped smile to match. She looked energetic in blue jeans, white gym shoes, thick orange socks and a seductively filled duck-egg blue sleeveless cashmere sweater.

Eric suggested that we go bowling and Gwen agreed. The jukebox blurted Englebert Humperdink while Eric rumbled fast-balls down the alley. Gwen was bored. I could tell from that puffed up, vexed opacity that girls get when they're letting you know they'd rather be some place else.

We gravitated back to the fountain. Jack, Ked, Franes and Eddie were all there, looking glass-eyed and vague. Jack winked conspiratorially.

'Wanna buy a four way?'

'A what?'

'A four way. Tab. Of Acid. LSD.'

I was alarmed. This was definitely forbidden territory.

'How much?' asked Eric.

'Four ways, four bucks.' Jack assumed the patronising manner of a doctor who was trying to be patient with a slatternly village girl who had fallen pregnant to a randy member of the local gentry.

'You get a piece of blotting paper, right? There's a stain where the acid's on the paper. You cut that into four pieces for four trips.'

Jack gave Gwen a dead-cool been-to-the-mountain look and twined her curls with an outstretched finger. 'You in?'

Gwen didn't look puffed up any more.

'You should start with one way each. I'll have one. That's two.' He noticed me and Eric again. 'You guys in?'

Eric nodded. So did I.

We found Ked, Franes and Eddie camped in Ked's EH like three gurus having a silence festival. Once we were in the car, Jack fished a pair of scissors and a tiny piece of blotting paper from his jacket, then handed each of us a piece with the instruction to roll it on our tongues. He said that this produced the best effect.

We obeyed and waited for something to happen. We waited some more. Eric was getting restless and muttering about a rip-off.

'Be cool,' said Jack. 'It takes a while. Let's go for a drive.'

It was immediately obvious that Ked should be doing nothing of the sort. He managed to turn right off Bunda Street into East Row and was heading towards Mort Street where it intersected with Cooyong. The car kangaroo-hopped every time he changed gear.

'I want to get out,' cried Gwen.

Instead of stopping, Ked gunned the car into the intersection and the seven of us were flung sideways by the car that hit our right rear end.

Ked panicked. 'Get out! Get out!'

We needed no prompting. Franes and Jack took off back the way we had come. Eddie vanished. Eric, Gwen and I found ourselves racing along the home stretch to my place. We laughed as we ran, our adrenalin pumping. When we slowed to regain our breath, we noticed things changing.

I suddenly had an exhilarating clarity of vision. We slowed to a dawdle to appreciate the effect of moonlight on silver-threaded leaves and the chirrups and murmurs of the night. I could see the insects chewing on the trees. I could see the fates of the night birds as they called us to travel with them through their star-bright domain.

Eric started his rave about life beyond earth.

'Look at those stars! Majestic Milky Way! Ian, you must admit it's mathematically impossible that the only intelligent life in the universe exists on this planet.'

I had my arm around Gwen and was barely listening.

'Come on, Ian. Say something sensible for once in your life!'

'Wow. I'm stoned.'

We entered my house stealthily, but needn't have bothered. The place was empty.

Up the spiral staircase and into my room. Where was Eric? It didn't matter. Gwen and I sat on my bed and started kissing deeply. We lay down so we could explore more of each other's body. This was much more delicious than speculating about life in the Milky Way. I was rigid with lust. Gwen rubbed at me with a cool half-smile that said she knew it wouldn't be long before she made me explode.

Then Eric waltzed in with a cup of coffee and a stage-polite good evening, oh, sorry to spoil the fun. He gave Gwen an appreciative perve as she hurried herself together.

'Wanna sip?' He held out his cup to her. 'Or I could make you one.'

Gwen gave Eric a glare and said she'd make it herself thank you very much. She made for the kitchen and we heard the clap of cupboards as she searched for a cup.

My blood swirled with interrupted lust.

'You stupid bastard.'

'Sorry about that,' he said, far from it. 'So what d'you think of the acid? Reckon I might try a two-way next time.'

Apart from an unsuccessful visit to Gwen's house when all I got to do was wait while she changed for netball, I saw nothing of her for weeks. Finally she appeared at the inter-school athletics carnival. She was representing her school in sprinting, relays and long jump. I was McDonald's second-string 800 metres man. Jack Winters was in the mile.

Gwen stayed close to her team and I barely got to say hello before the lunch break. When lunch time came, so did Jack. All three of us found a spot under a tree. I went to get a pie and when I returned Gwen had her arms around Jack and they were kissing. It seemed that Jack's charisma was infectious.

I won my race that day. I ran with purpose and balance. I shut Gwen out of my mind and ran perfectly. Then I gathered my gear and headed home.

My path took me past the CCEGS girls. Gwen had seen my feat and was trying a guilty smile of congratulations. I gave her a stony look and strode out of her life.

In 1972 my family moved again.

'Hall!' we chorused in disbelief.

This time Don, Amy and I had allies. Nadine and Carole hated the idea of another uprooting as much as we did.

Paul defended the proposed fifty acres near Hall. He said that our mother needed a bigger place for the dogs.

'*My* mother lives in London,' said Nadine, a comment calculated to make everybody cringe.

But Paul had a point. Now all of us kids were well into our teens, Mum had been casting about for other creatures to nurture. She'd taken up breeding Labrador retrievers. Paul had turned the back yard into a concreted run for the dozen or so dogs she'd collected so far, but neighbours, particularly the Maxwells, were whingeing about the barking. We'd received a nasty letter from the Department of the Capital Territory.

'Why Hall?' Nadine persisted. 'It's so far ...'

'Nadine,' said Paul, as if the matter was settled and she'd be wise to stop her bitching, 'you have a driver's licence and a car.'

'But I'll end up driving everybody to school.' Nadine was in her final year at Watson. She was school captain and was planning a degree in law. 'Father, I haven't the time to play chauffeur.'

Paul pointed at me. 'Ian's nearly seventeen. He'll soon have his licence and I'll be buying a Kombi van so your Mum can take the dogs to weekend shows. Ian can use that to take people to school. And if he has things to do, he can keep the Kombi and you can pick everyone else up. And there's a bus that stops outside McDonald High and runs all the way to Hall.'

That silenced any complaints I might have had. The

thought of having wheels at my disposal put a whole new perspective on things.

But Nadine decided she wasn't finished. 'As soon as I've finished school I'm leaving this ghastly country.'

Paul gave a snort of derision at this proclamation. To his subsequent sorrow, because Nadine did exactly that.

I must admit I quite liked living on our new property. Except for the Shit Run. The Shit Run was horrible.

We moved in mid-winter. The five of us kids would get up at dawn and wriggle blearily into every item of warm clothing we owned. Then we'd pile into the Kombi with me at the wheel learning accelerator/clutch co-ordination on the journey across the paddocks to the kennels.

It was so cold we had to remember to leave the hose running downhill so the water wouldn't freeze inside it at night. As a precaution, we'd bring hot water with us in case the tap was frozen solid.

Once we had a decent flow of water, Nadine would start hosing down the topmost kennels while Don and I brandished stiff brooms, sweeping away the previous day's aggregation of dog shit. We'd work in shuddering silence, with Amy and Carole bringing up the rear feeding the dogs so that they could make more shit. Sometimes Nadine would accidentally-on-purpose spray Don or me with frigid water just for the malicious fun of seeing us freeze our nuts off all together.

The terrible chore completed, we'd go home to take turns showering. Sometimes it was so cold I preferred not to shower at all, washing up instead at the kitchen sink. We'd huddle in front of the big range fire while Mum made breakfast. Then off we'd go to school, paranoid that we smelt like turds.

Eric and I were studying the same subjects – English, Ancient and Modern History, Geography and Biology – so it was simple enough to get out of the Shit Run. Every chance I had I'd invent a collaboration and stay a night or weekend at Eric's. We'd hit the books at the Kingston Library or in the enormous reading room at the National Library by the lake.

But there was no studying done on Saturday nights. These were reserved exclusively for recreational debauchery.

Now and then we'd gatecrash a party and get pissed on beer and wine while listening to music like Jethro Tull's 'Aqualung'. More frequently, we'd buy a few joints or a flask of vodka and head to the Kingston Coffee House.

It wasn't really a coffee house, more like a big loft in a church community hall. Some liberal-thinking folk had decided it would do well as a place where young people could gather for music, chess, coffee and raisin toast. Smoking was okay but drugs and alcohol were not allowed. No problem! We'd get stoned or drunk before we went in.

One night we were at the coffee house gazing blearily through the smoke haze when Eric nudged me in the ribs. 'There's a familiar face.'

Quite a pretty one, too, if you liked the ethereal Twiggy look.

'That's Elaine Cronin, you dope. She's in our English class.'

We made our way to where Elaine was sitting cross-legged with a coffee, a cigarette and a paperback copy of *A Clockwork Orange*. She put down the book.

'Hi.' She gave Eric a smile to let him know he'd been noted and approved.

Which was all the encouragement Eric needed to give me a look to let me know that it would be a good idea for me to piss off and make my own entertainment.

So I took Mike Stanton on in a game of chess, looking up now and then to see Eric and Elaine deep in talk. Eric looked more animated than I had ever seen him.

Heading back to Eric's house afterwards, I ventured the obvious. 'You two seemed to hit it off.'

'You could say that,' said Eric. 'We're going out next weekend.'

I considered this for a moment.

'And I suppose you won't be needing a chauffeur.'

'Elaine has her licence; I have my learner's. We'll borrow Mum's Mini.'

As usual, I spent the night on a blow-up mattress on Eric's bedroom floor. He fell asleep immediately, dreaming, no doubt, of the rendezvous to come.

I tossed and turned and couldn't sleep. Something niggled at my brain, seeping through from a dark place of forgotten memories.

The world was shifting once again. And this time it was taking Eric into territory where I could not follow.

The school play for the year was *HMS Pinafore*. I was playing Dick Deadeye, and Irina Davis was playing Mrs Buttercup.

Irina was blonde, wholesome and entirely uncorrupted. She sang beautifully, and held the harmonies in a way that carried the musical semi-literates like me and Able Seaman Eric, who struggled to hold a tune at all.

Now that Eric was happily romancing Elaine Cronin, and I was alone, I found myself observing the budding of love everywhere I looked among my Fifth Form theatrical shipmates. Except for Irina. There she'd be at dress rehearsals, alone in the wings, ready to take her cue and dispense her Dutch-mother bonhomie on centre stage. She seemed to be lonely too. So, when the cast got together after our run of performances and I'd had a few too many spiked glasses of punch, I asked her to the Sixth Form farewell dance and she accepted.

The farewell day began well enough. Irina's parents welcomed me and the other members of the Fifth Form Social Committee with champagne and orange juice in their back yard. They smiled indulgently as we armed ourselves with water pistols, flour bombs and streamers with which to help the departing Sixth Formers redecorate the school. I doubt if they'd have condoned our plan to steal the Centurion tank parked outside the War Memorial, but it didn't happen anyway, because the motor was disabled and the hatches were welded shut.

When we got to school we made a huge mess with the flour bombs. The headmaster kicked everyone off campus, and we regrouped for an afternoon at the Rex hotel.

Back at Eric's we showered and spruced up. I climbed into my brand new forest-green Stafford Ellinson two-piece suit, already a little unsteady on my pins but merrily determined to continue the good time.

Outside the assembly hall we could hear the band warming up. Eric and I skulled a hip-flask of vodka and went inside to meet the girls.

Irina was dressed like she was going to a 1960s American high school Homecoming Dance, all satiny and pink and perfect.

'You look nice,' I said, and even as she smiled appreciatively I knew I hadn't really delivered a compliment. She looked so conservative! Maybe I'd already had too much to drink. There was trouble brewing in my mental circuits. As soon as the band struck up I hauled Irina onto the floor and flung her about carelessly, lurching anarchically as if she wasn't there.

'Ian,' she said politely, clearly uncomfortable, 'maybe we should help with the drinks.'

This was my duty, but my brain cells were dying by the thousands.

'Nah! You go. I'll catch up with you.'

I didn't. Vaguely aware of Irina making a brave face as she watched me from the servery, I danced with the delicious, unreachable Clare Campbell and the curvy Alexandra Marks. Then somehow I ended up dancing with Wendy Woodcroft.

. Wendy was small for a young woman about to face the adult world, with long braided black hair, big-eyes, quirking lips and a hyper-direct attitude. She suggested we go parking.

So, while I created no scene with Irina at the dance, I sowed the seeds for a real beauty afterwards by leaving the dance with Wendy, hand-in-hand and full of voluptuous intent.

Wendy and I decided to go to the after-dance party first. I can barely remember the house where it was held, except that it was dimly lit and vibrating with music.

Jack Winters was there with all the other freaks, off their faces in a dope haze. There was a nine-gallon keg and a stack of plastic glasses. Eric and Elaine arrived with Mad Mac Dowdle and Dick Evanston. We set about getting smashed. By the time Irina turned up, I was extremely drunk.

She came with Di Spring, Graham Burbridge and Simone Simpson, and seemed determined not to get upset when she saw me with Wendy. But she must have told the others what had happened, because Graham was looking upset enough for two. He came striding over, towering into the haze, furious.

'You are an utter fucking bastard,' came his growling greeting.

I peered at him unsteadily and said nothing.

'I should beat the crap out of you now, but you're too pissed to fart.'

He leaned down to make sure I got the next bit. 'So, shithead, I'll be waiting. I'm gonna get you for this.'

He gave me a short-arm jab in the guts to go on with, then turned and left me lurching. I grabbed Eric's sleeve to keep from falling over.

'I'd say you're in a spot of strife,' Eric observed, in his usual sympathetic manner. 'Perhaps you should suicide now. Die with honour.' He thrust a brimming plastic glass in my hand. I spilled half of it on the carpet. Someone put on a Credence album and Wendy made me dance. I lost myself in them old cotton fields down south. Then I found my thrill on Blueberry Hill as Wendy held me close and gyrated all over me.

We went parking by the Molonglo River. The grassy places between the weeping willows were occupied by other couples, everyone going hard at it.

It was cold, but Wendy was warm as she undid her blouse and rubbed her hard little nipples against my lips. This was no teen dream. My chance had arrived.

And it promptly abandoned me again. The flesh was flaccid. My spirit became desperate, then humbled. My penis felt about the size of a cigarette.

'This is ridiculous,' said Wendy. 'Take me home.'

Her eyes glared accusingly through the dark. My shame was a beacon.

I had seen brighter times.

Having decided that ceremonial suicide would be an over-reaction, Eric advised karate lessons.

But Graham left me alone. For the past several years he'd been dating Simone Simpson but he was now seriously involved with Di Spring. He was also enrolling for university and he had a vacation job on a building site in Belconnen. Graham was starting his adult life, and I was reprieved.

This mercy was of little immediate value. I was to be further depressed by my incapacity with women.

The immaculate young body of Ginnie Kaspreson presented itself near-naked on the sandy sunlit bank of the Queanbeyan River. We had wandered away from a party at Mick Major's place, leaving the rest of the party goers stoned supine on the carpet. Ginnie was seriously beautiful, and I blew it.

Literally.

I was ready for some easy rest and relaxation by the time we escaped to Thailand for our annual holiday. And, as fate would have it, I was aided in my quest by an unexpected bounty.

I was coming out of the Saigon Bakery on Silom Road not far from Patpong and was hooking into the first in a personal feast of their brain-blasting chocolate mousse eclairs when a man almost shirtfronted me.

He had brown thonged feet, a scrawny frame in dirty blue jeans and a cheap cotton T-shirt, a matted thatch of hair and a scrappy black beard. The man was clutching a cheap plastic airline bag; paranoia in his face. He gestured with the bag.

'You like smoke?' he asked with a French accent.

I'd never seen the guy in my life. After recent incidents of Thai cops getting narky with hippies, I wasn't saying a word.

I took another bite of eclair and kept walking. He followed.

'Here, take a look!' He tried to thrust his bag into my hands. 'What are you fear of? I am not the police. Come to the reality, man, take a look!'

He hauled me into a narrow space between two buildings. 'Take a look.' He flapped open the bag so I could see the stash of dope, partly wrapped in newspaper. There were maybe six or seven ounces of big, resin-crusted heads.

'You want the ganja?'

I hesitated. He gave an impatient roll of the eyes and patted my shoulder.

'It is yours for no charge. Come, you desire it.'

This was true enough. The bag contained top-shelf dope.

'Yes, man! I take the train tonight. I go to Penang.'

My reservations evaporated. The guy would spend half his life in jail if he was caught holding drugs at Haadyai, or, worse, on the Malaysian side. The Malays hated hippies even more than the Thais did. I took the parcel and stashed it in the army surplus haversack that usually toted my textbooks.

The Frenchman beamed. 'I could tell you were the one. I trust your face.'

He accepted one of my precious eclairs with the relish of a gourmand and waved away, off to his train.

I made a fair dent in the Frenchman's contraband before it came time to fly home. I was stoned night and day. Dad certainly noticed, but he said nothing. At the airport he shot me a glance that seemed to ask, 'You're not taking that stuff home with you, are you?'

And my reassuring look could have been interpreted as saying, 'Well, at least this time the cargo's not explosive.'

I had first noticed Simone Simpson on a Third Form geography excursion to Mount Kosciusko. Simone had been standing there among the tarns in her ribbed tights, tartan skirt, bulky white jumper and long black hair, framed by cirques and the distant glacial valley. A sharp little pain of admiration had shivered through my heart.

During the sunset ride home, with the cabin lights red-gold low and the radio playing the Mamas and the Papas' 'Dream a Little Dream of Me', I looked back at Simone from my seat down the front. She was sharing a silly secret with Ann-Maree Franklin and laughing with her perfect teeth and red lips. Her eyes found me watching and she gave me a smile and a little share of the laugh. I had cherished it all the way home.

When Simone started going out with Graham Burbridge my hopes were smashed. But now Graham was dating Di Spring and the coast was clear.

As we began our matriculation year at McDonald High, I waited for my chance to approach Simone. When it didn't come, I enlisted Eric in a conspiracy.

'Ask her to the movies,' I demanded.

'What?'

'Ask her to the movies. I'll ask Ann-Maree. Come on,

Eric. I'm *dying* for that girl!'

'Ask her yourself.'

'She'll say no.'

'Do you suppose Simone is stupid? She knows I'm going with Elaine.'

'Say you had a fight. Then when we're together, I'll move in on Simone and there'll be no damage done.'

'What about Ann-Maree?'

'You can drive her home. Buy her a hot chocolate or something. I'll pay.'

'Ian, this is pretty low.'

'Come on, Eric. I'm desperate!'

'You can say that again.'

It worked. We went to see *Cabaret* at the Manuka Theatre. My Marella jubes and I sat between Ann-Maree and Simone, with Eric on Simone's right. When the lights dimmed I leaned over and put my shoulder close to Simone's so that when she moved she'd brush against me.

For a long time nothing happened. I moved closer. This time, she felt my presence and eased against me so I could feel her warmth. Then she put her hand on my knee and, thinking that this had to be heaven, I took it.

After the show we all had coffee. The three of them shared knowing smirks and I demanded to know what was going on.

'You know,' said Simone, 'you could have asked me. I would have said yes.'

Eric gave me his crookedest grin. I wanted to clobber him.

One thing you have to admit about John Donne and Shakespeare is that they were not too rotten at getting words to take the reader journeying along with them. I discovered the difficulty of this task as my own poems lumbered and lurched toward a distant personal Bethlehem to be born.

The start of my poetry writing coincided with Simone Simpson. I sought inspiration from the poets but found it in her.

We sat together in English and Ancient History. It was hard to defy the distractions of her proximity at those intimate double desks, but with Simone's help I started pulling in marks that startled those who'd pegged me as a slack-arse satisfied merely with passes.

I found myself foregoing the recess smoko up the hill in order to stay in Simone's company. Apart from the five-cent pontoon freaks, this meant that I was just about the only bloke in the senior common room.

At lunch Simone would give me her home-made sandwiches: thick buttered crusty white bread with tangy matured cheddar, juicy sliced tomatoes and salt. She said I needed fattening up and she didn't. Later on, she'd sun long brown legs with her girlfriends on the grassy bank overlooking the oval, watching us boys trying to boot the bladder out of the footy. I'd walk her back to class to breathe her scent again, feeling dizzy and strangely centred at the same time.

One afternoon Simone walked past the muddy members of the senior hockey team, going home after a session in the library. I begged the coach to be excused and raced after her, offering to carry her books. Simone rewarded me by asking me in for hot chocolate.

Her parents were nice English people. Her house was immaculate and decorated with taste and restraint. The gardens were slaved over by Simone's proudly green-thumbed father, who stood smoking a pipe among his roses in the twilight as we walked up. I staggered beneath the burden of book bags and hockey stick, my school-tie holding my hair in some sort of order and my knees muddy from the chase of the practice pitch. Simone was leggy and demure in her full-buttoned white blouse and tartan skirt.

When I met Simone's mum I could see where her daughters got their stunning looks from. She gave me a sweet steaming mug of hot chocolate, over which I chattered politely and behaved admirably. Mrs Simpson let it be known that she'd approve of a further visit from my good self, perhaps before I went romping on the hockey field again.

Next time I was resplendent in school uniform, with my hair combed back into a presentable pony tail. I even had the gall to pinch a rose from a handy garden outcrop and offer it to Mrs Simpson as a serious tribute to my civilisation. I was invited to stay for dinner.

Mr Simpson came in from the yard, fired up his pipe and offered me a glass of dinner ale. He went to a crystal-fronted cabinet and took out two tall handled glasses etched with the Bristol Rovers' coat-of-arms. He poured full glasses and the froth tickled my upper lip as we said cheers and took a quaff.

'Hits the spot, eh lad?'

'Certainly does!' I said with gusto.

'You share Simone's classes.'

'Some of them.'

'She says you're quite a help.'

'I think it might be the other way round, sir.'

'That's good to hear. I'd like her to get into the CCAE.'

'I reckon she'll get early admission to ANU as well as the college. We find out in the next few weeks.'

'That your direction then, son?'

'I think so. I thought I'd have a go at Anthropology and Asian Studies.'

This was the first time I'd suggested that to anybody, let alone myself, but it had a good ring to it. And it would be topical – Labor had won the 1972 election and our troops were home at last from Vietnam.

'Friendships in Asia will soon be more important than keeping enemies.'

Mr Simpson nodded gravely and tugged at his pipe. Then he hit me with the question I knew was coming.

'What do you think of this pot thing, cannabis?'

'I have nothing philosophically against it, sir. But I prefer to concentrate on my studies right now.' I waved my near-empty glass. 'A beer is fine with me.'

He grunted with suspicion, as if he reckoned my answer might be as pat as it sounded.

Simone came to the rescue, claiming that we had to work on an assignment due the next day. I drained my beer in a gulp as Simone force-marched me to her room.

'For God's sake,' she whispered as we reached her doorway, 'don't talk about smoking or dope or boozing.'

She led me into her chamber. The desk was covered with personal treasures, her bed strewn with books. She lit some jasmine incense sticks and closed the door. Then she sat me on the bed and pulled up a chair so that she had her thighs straddled around my knees.

'Teach me.'

I bent down to kiss her face, her forehead, her eyes, her ears. I cupped her in my hands, tongue on lips and tingling teeth.

We heard soft footsteps in the carpet corridor and sprang apart. A tap on the door then it opened swiftly to reveal the droll languid smile of Simone's older sister.

'You've not too long to dinner. Mum's just turned the heat up.'

Mercifully I was allowed to confine myself to small talk at dinner. I boasted of my sporting prowess as a fleet-footed inside-left, the scorer of class-act goals for McDonald's senior side, and praised Mrs Simpson's tender lamb roast with home-made mint sauce and a crusty hint of garlic. Upon tucking boisterously into seconds, I felt the barrier to admission to the Simpson circle lifting.

When the time came to say goodbye, Mrs Simpson told me I was welcome to visit Simone any time during daylight hours and that we could study together until half-past ten at night.

'You've made a bit of a hit,' said Simone, as I prepared to climb aboard the Kombi. 'But you'd better be on your best behaviour.'

Then she demolished me by giving my groin a suggestive rub. I drove back to Hall in an agony of love and lust.

And vowed to lay off dope and bingeing. I'd have done anything for the sake of Simone Simpson.

Don and Amy had great laughs over my lunacy. They said I was moon sick. They swooned about melodramatically and blew each other outlandish kisses and pretended to throw confetti.

Strangely, Eric seemed sullened by the whole affair. It was as if he was jealous that I'd found someone whose attention I wanted more than his.

As my scholarship continued its exponential improvement, Eric's began to decline. He started spending class-time reading a paperback Heinlein or Bradbury hidden under his desk.

Was he sulking? Were things not going so well with him and Elaine? I didn't much care. Simone had become my universe.

Simone and I conspired for our chance to make love.

The opportunity arose during term break. Simone had a cousin in Sydney who she hadn't seen for ages. She used some savings and took the train to visit her.

I tried to persuade Eric to hitch-hike with me, but he grumpily replied that he didn't feel like it.

So I went with Peter Warrensgate. His brother was at

Sydney Uni and he rented a boarding-house room in Cremorne. He'd given Pete a duplicate key.

We made it to Goulburn in good time, but we were caught in a downpour crossing to the Sydney side of the long Goulburn bridge. We had to hunker in the hang-over drizzle, waiting for rides. It was twilight by the time we reached Liverpool. We took a train to Central Station, mesmerised by the flashpast of headlights stopped at boomgate intersections.

The boarding house was a mansion once splendid, now ramshackle and dark. The room was tiny. It barely enclosed a single bed, a table and chair, a water jug and wash-basin, a cold-water sink and a single gas ring. Someone had built a shelf over one corner to store winter clothes and luggage, and a bookshelf with bricks. The bookshelf held a dozen or so paperbacks and a bulky pile of texts on structural engineering. On the table were some fancy brass instruments for technical drawing and a thick pad of works-in-progress. The whole room was lit by a single lamp, which illuminated a big Paul Klee poster. Quite a pleasing scene, almost romantic. Even if the bed was small.

We had the rest of the night and all the next day to kill before we met Simone at Circular Quay. We blew some dope and headed for the dismal dining room to see if we could scrounge some food. We passed a lounge with vast dusty armchairs and little wizened old people sheltering beneath their bulky woollen blankets while watching coin-in-the-slot telly.

An ancient crone emerged from the kitchen to inform us that we were too late for dinner.

We found a fish and chip shop and ordered flake with chips and vinegar. We guzzled it down on a bench overlooking the harbour, blowing Thailand's finest in much mellowment.

From all his tossing around in his brother's bed that night, I figured Pete was either bloody uncomfortable or beset in his dreams by demons from hell. I slept spread diagonally across the floor. My dreams promised heaven.

Next morning we joined early commuters on the Cremorne ferry and sat with the rising sun thawing the chill of dawn from our stiffened bones. We had a beer in a white-tile derro pub that smelled of slop-sodden runners and disinfectant and poor old pissed bastards.

Things improved further into town. The rubbish-strewn alleys were replaced by arcades and coffee shops scented by freshly ground Java. We loitered over our cups and bought ourselves a packet of Gauloises to share as a special treat. Then we took in a movie, *The Man in the Glass Booth*. We rummaged in a second-hand book shop and I bought a book called *Siddhartha*.

The lady at the counter looked like a motherly hippie.

'Bit of a seeker, are you?' she asked me as I paid for the book.

I had no idea what she was talking about, but I nodded and gave her a bland smile.

'You'll like that one, then.'

I exited with Pete laughing at my heels.

'Seeker. I know what you seek!'

He evaded the swipe I aimed at the middle of his cowardly fleeing back and hastened away in full guffaw.

I gave chase and clobbered him with my haversack. He kept laughing.

Simone turned up on time. Pete colluded by saying he had a rendezvous to keep. I think he went to another movie. Simone and I crossed the harbour together, with our arms close around each other in the whip of the evening sea-breeze.

We made love in the cramp of the boarding-house bed. I was inexpert and clumsy. Simone soothed me and I was able to calm down and allow myself to be enveloped in her perfection. United, we came before God.

That's if He ever stopped planning global pratfall long enough to notice us. Just long enough to bestow upon us a little continued bliss on this lovers' first night. But no.

There was a key in the door and we found ourselves confronted by an astonished young man who could only have been Pete's older brother.

'Ahem,' said I.

'Hi there,' said Simone.

He stepped inside and closed the door. 'Who are you?'

'Pete's friends,' I blurted. 'Up from Canberra.'

'Oh,' he said mildly, as if his universe was now back in order. 'That's all right then.'

He gave Simone an agreeable smile. 'I was just about to make a cuppa. I think I could find a couple more cups.'

Simone called up all her reserves of British normalcy and said that would be nice, but would he mind just turning away a little while she dressed. He obliged.

'Bit of a surprise, I must say.'

I managed the feeble observation that I supposed it would be. Simone said she was sorry about the intrusion.

'That's okay. I'm sure you would've made the bed. I'm afraid you can't stay, though.'

As if we intended to!

We went through the absurdity of instant coffee, mine in a jar, giving the brother the latest on Pete while his eyes roved from Simone to the delicious crumplement of his bed. Dirty bastard! I couldn't get her out of there quick enough.

We ended up at her cousin's place in the dead of night, after what seemed like hours on the train.

Simone tapped on a window and a light came on. A face appeared blinking into the gloom.

'It's me, let us in,' whispered Simone.

The curtains swished shut and I was led to a side door which opened with a stealthy crink of springs.

The cousin saw me. 'Oh, no. He can't come in.'

Simone tried to argue, but I was doomed.

'I'd be out of here if I were you, before you get Simone and me in trouble.'

I slunk off into the night.

My step-father, Paul, the very busy and very respectable suburban GP, was arrested and charged with performing an illegal abortion. I found out about it when I went into a milk bar near school and saw Paul's picture and a screaming headline splashed all over page one of the afternoon daily.

All the way home to Hall we speculated fearfully. When we got there, Mum had to field the questions because Paul was in Canberra meeting his lawyers. She told us that he had given evidence that some policemen had bashed a prisoner in the cells. Paul thought that the charges against him were a way for the police to get revenge.

'Did he do it?'

'Of course not!'

'What about the practice?' Don wanted to know.

'Since the paper came out, he's seen two patients. He'll be lucky to get any tomorrow.'

I was only allowed in court on the day that I was called to give evidence. I had my hair cut conservatively short for the occasion.

I was able to provide a partial alibi, but it was Amy, who'd been helping out at Paul's surgery on the day in question, who proved to the magistrate's satisfaction that the charges did not stand up.

The report of the no-case-to-answer verdict was buried on an inside page. You would have needed a magnifying glass to read it. Paul's patients did not return.

Eric wagged school and listened to every word at the committal.

'Had to keep an eye on what was going on. You know. Guilty or not guilty.'

'What's that supposed to mean?'

'I heard all the evidence, Ian. You just rehearsed your lines.'

When his absence was noticed Eric was dragged before the headmaster, who gave him a week-long suspension. That seemed bloody stupid to me, because the only way Eric was going to catch up on his work was to be in class instead of exiled from it. But it didn't seem to bother Eric. There was a distance and indifference about him that mystified me.

One afternoon during his suspension I saw Eric watching the white-and-grey tartan flood leaving school. He was leaning against a gum tree on the other side of the car-clogged crescent that passed McDonald High.

From a distance it looked like he was unwell. I went over to him.

'What's with you? You look like you're half asleep.'

He gave me a leering semi-conscious grin.

'Just holding up the tree.' He tried to wave me off with contempt but nearly fell over with the effort of his gesture.

'What the hell are you on?'

He grinned again, and exuded guilt mixed with primal glee.

'Smack. Man, I smoked smack.'

He mumbled something about it being awesome. It didn't look too awesome to me. My friend was nearly senseless. I dragged him to the Kombi, hauled him into the passenger seat and listened to his laboured semi-catatonic babbling as we waited for Don, Carole and Amy to turn up.

I swore them all to secrecy and we detoured to Eric's

place. Thankfully his mother was still at work. I chucked him into bed with instructions to sleep it off, which he promptly started to do.

The next morning Eric called to say thanks.

'Man, that is heavy stuff.'

'Maybe you should leave it alone.'

'Bullshit. If you get so high just smoking . . .'

'Don't even say it, Eric!' I used my most serious voice, and I bloody meant it, too. 'Don't do it.'

There was a silence.

'Where'd you get it?'

More silence.

'Elaine?'

No answer.

'Eric, for Christ's sake. Do yourself a favour and leave it alone.'

At last a response. 'Yeah, you're right.'

'I know I am.' I let this sink in. 'You back at school next Monday?'

'Yeah.'

There was not even a distant hint of enthusiasm.

'I need to talk to you.'

There was fear and urgency in Simone's voice. It terrified me. She looked at the common-room clock and shook her head.

'There isn't time now. Recess. Meet me here. I have to go.'

I had double Geography. I didn't hear a word Mr Creed

said. I considered the dreadful possibilities. And with a gasp I realised that Simone must be pregnant. Everyone looked at me as I sputtered and stared, blank with inner terror.

It's a funny thing. If you only knew it at the time, seemingly meaningless things can be an oracle of your fate.

I was skidding along the lino tiles making record time for the common room when Mr Cockson, the Maths master, came striding out of a classroom. There was no time to avoid a collision. A sheaf of test papers went slithering as they hit the floor. Hastily I gathered them up and handed them back.

'Sorry, sir.'

I tried to scuttle off.

'Come here, McDermott.'

I obeyed, and observed again the face of the man who had humbled me. The man who back in 1970 had drawn himself to his full Army-Reserve-Captain-and-Leader-of-Cadets height and, in the middle of an algebra test, had roared at me to surrender my Vietnam Moratorium badge.

'Running in the corridors is prohibited.'

'Yes sir, but I was in a hurry. Sorry.'

'You'd better pick up papers in the quadrangle.'

This was an insult. The bullying bastard knew I was a prefect and that I would be in for a double dose of humiliation.

'Sir,' I said, seeking a little dignity, 'I'll do lunch patrol if you prefer.'

'Papers. Now!'

I obeyed again. But after making myself visible for thirty

seconds of paper collecting, I desperately detoured and found Simone.

She looked lost and defeated. She was pregnant for sure. I had an appalling vision of needing to seek Paul's help, and immediately felt an unutterable swine that that was my first reaction.

'I'm not allowed to see you any more.'

I shook my head in stunned denial. She nodded, trembling, shatteringly gorgeous.

'It's true. Mum found out you were dealing dope.'

The enormity of the situation sank in.

'Mr Cockson told Mum he had an obligation to protect me. He said he hadn't said anything before because he thought I'd have dropped you by now.'

I wanted to find Cockson and beat his brains in. I looked towards the common-room door in the hope that he might be passing.

'Who told Cockson?'

She shrugged and shook her head. She took both my hands in hers.

'Look, we're going to have to cool it for a while.'

'I barely even touch the stuff any more! You told me to behave myself and I have been. Simone, I love you.'

My fervour attracted the attention of everyone in the common room. Simone stroked my hand and held it. But she wasn't backing down. 'You can't come over any more.'

'Then you'll have to come to me.'

Simone examined my soul.

'I suppose I will.'

Our out-of-school existence became clandestine. We would sail into the safe haven of the Kingston Coffee Shop, smooching and groping in the dimly lit cushioned corners.

Some nights Simone would tell her parents that she was staying with girlfriends. We turned Nadine's recently vacated bedroom at Hall into a sanctuary of LPs and sentimental Saturday night movies. The music swung to the metronome of our bodies. Time beyond this room became a countdown of days-to-go before we returned to it. It was our blissful pleasure dome, built for the eternity of our love.

Eric made himself scarce. I put it down to diplomacy, but when he did turn up one night, I could see that he had mainlined.

There was a serenity about him. This time his eyes were clear and calm.

'You shot up.'

He nodded with nonchalance. There was no guilt in his gaze this time. Eric Masters was in control.

I knew this was something Eric wanted to talk about. But Simone clucked her disapproval, so I just shrugged.

'If that's what you want to do, man.'

There was an eclipse in Eric's eyes.

Elaine Cronin must have been a junkie. But I was so engrossed in Simone, I did not confront Eric again about what he was doing, not even when he scratched a mozzie bite inside his wrist and I saw purple needle tracks all the way up his arm. Not even when I saw that misty guilty smile. Not even when I saw that Eric and Elaine were looking thin. And sometimes sick.

Just before the HSC exams, Elaine stopped coming to school. There was no explanation, official or gossiped. Her desk was cleared out by a couple of prefects. For all I knew, she might have OD'd.

Eric didn't talk about it, and, of course, I didn't ask. He withdrew impenetrably.

With the fortnight of final exams looming close, my girl and I were among the dozens lined up in echoing silence along the reading-room table in the National Library. Eric hung around the front, dragging on Camel Filters and looking out over the lake towards Mount Ainslie. Perhaps he was thinking of happier days. Days before he did drugs.

When the exams arrived, I was bloody near smug. Simone was nervous, but she hauled good marks and ended up being offered so many uni places she got nervous all over again, trying to decide which one she wanted. I breezed every paper and dragged down four level ones and a this-student-could-do-better-but-he-passed in Biology, the friendly science. Eric fronted up to the exam hall and left early every time. He passed all the same.

We all got pissed on champagne and orange juice just as we had the year before. We armed ourselves with flour bombs and streamers and bedecked the school we were about to leave forever. Again the headmaster chucked us out and again we made our way to the Rex hotel, supreme school-yard seniors no more.

Simone tried to defy her parents.

While Amy and Don went ahead to Thailand, I stayed in Canberra landscaping a carpark at the Woden Town Centre. Simone took on a casual public service job. The two of us were saving for Simone's fare to Bangkok.

We flew to Thailand just after Christmas. Simone immediately contracted a crippling case of gastro and was laid flat for a week.

Even after she'd recovered, her vacation held little joy. The mail delivered no forgiving words from Canberra. Simone feared that when she returned home it would be to pack and leave for good.

Paul's business had not recovered from the abortion scandal, and he'd been forced to sell up. He and Mum had purchased a place just north of Brisbane, in a growing rural-urban subdivision called Kallangur. The place had boarding kennels which would earn them money while Paul tried to build a new practice. Mum wrote that it was a big place and that, yes, there was a room for Simone if she wanted it.

Simone hated Kallangur from the moment she saw it. The property was a dusty triangular ten acres bordered on one side by the northern railway, on another by a motor racing circuit, on the third by a dairy farm. The boarding kennels reeked of dog shit and demanded renovations which Paul could not afford. The house was old, wood and fibro, a humid haven for insects that were unheard of in the temperate suburban sensibility of Canberra.

I can still picture Simone trying to wash her hair under a tap that offered a grubby pressureless trickle of dam water. I can see her pretty face wrinkled with disgust at the fly-specks and cockroaches and cobwebs; her brow beaded with sweat. The hammering heat in that sweltering summer of monsoonal floods seemed sent to torment her by way of parental vengeance.

Mum tried to be welcoming, but every time I laid eyes on Simone I wanted to cringe because she was. I was withered by her disappointment.

She deferred her university enrolment and found a job splicing movies at Channel Ten. I'd drop her at Mount Coot-tha on the way to my university lectures at St Lucia and pick her up on the way home.

After a week or so, Simone announced that she had found a room-mate and was moving out the next day.

'Jesus, Simone! What about us?'

'Ian, you know I love you. But tonight is absolutely the last time I'm setting foot in this horrible place.'

The most heart-rending sound in the world is that of a suitcase clacking shut.

Soon after this, I got a letter from Eric.

Ian
I'm not ready for another stretch of school. Twelve years is long

enough without a break. In any case, I'm stuffed if I know what I want or where I'm going. Except that I'm coming up to Queensland to say g'day. Mum's given me the big Toyota. I'll be there in a week.

Eric

'Simone,' I said, 'lets go back to Canberra with Eric.'

'You're dropping out?'

I nodded.

'Are you sure that's a good idea?'

'I don't even know what I'm doing there.'

'What about our plans? I'm making good money. We could get our own place soon.'

'Let's do it in Canberra.'

'Ian, we can't just drop everything and go, just like that!'

'Why not?'

For the first time, Simone looked at me with dislike. 'It's giving up. Without a fight. It's not even trying.'

But the lure of her parents' rose garden must have been too strong. A day or so later, she called me at Kallangur.

'When is he leaving? I have to give notice.'

Not long after we returned to Canberra, Simone called me at Eric's place and asked me to meet her for coffee.

'I think we should take a break from each other.'

The hot confusion and fear flooded through me the way it had in the common room the year before. But this time it was Simone making the suggestion, not her parents, and that made it worse.

'All this bouncing about from here to Thailand to Brisbane and back to here. It's like I'm stopping you from doing anything with your life. And I'm getting nowhere myself.'

'Give me a chance, Simone! I'll get a job. We'll do fine here.'

'I was doing fine in Brisbane. I know it was my own decision to come back here, but now I need some time on my own to find out what I want.'

'Take it. But why does that mean we have to take a break from each other?'

'Because I'm not sure if I love you any more.'

Pissed stupid in the university union bar. The worm at the end of the bottle. Pints and jugs and deals in the carpark. Empty reaches of night and fog on the lake. Ghost-silver ripples laughing back at my desolation.

Fury on the hockey field. Mowing down the hapless Cordies. Scoring twice in the grudge match against Barton but a busted nose and blood all down my face from the punch. Butterfly stitches and beers with a dash of lime in the Scottish Bar. A hero. A drunkard. Lurching about on a Saturday night. The night that used to belong to me and Simone.

Bumping into Simone's sister and breathing fumes all over her. 'Say hi from me! Don't forget to say hi.' The insect says hi.

I met her at Lanyon Homestead in bright sunshine. We walked among the perfect rose gardens set among the outbuildings that were still redolent of the bloody years of the white men's civilising mission: the sheep runs and poisoned waterholes of *Terra Nullus*.

Our oneness was gone.

'I feel I have to ask your permission to touch you,' I told her.

'But I do still love you.'

And I did not. Yes I did. I didn't know. It was too soon to be letting go.

My hands in her hair as we kissed and cried.

Later that year, Eric was sacked by the *Canberra Times* for failing to verify the authors of a sheaf of letters to the editor.

The Chief of Staff found the yellowing missives in the bottom of a drawer and waved them accusingly at Eric, who accepted his marching orders with an expressionless shrug.

The Chief of Staff had also been on the warpath for me ever since I had left an urgent delivery for Sydney on the dashboard when I was doing the airport run. My second warning came when I let the car run dry of engine oil and the motor seized in the parking lot outside Parliament House. I'd pulled up to collect a batch of copy from the press gallery, more interested in whether I'd run into Gough Whitlam than the smoke coming out of the engine.

Knowing therefore that my dismissal was approaching faster than Gough's, and sick of being bullied by reporters demanding coffee and pizzas and yelling across the room when their copy was ready for the subs, I resigned in sympathy with Eric.

Simone was not impressed when I told her Eric and I were heading north.

'It's just a holiday. We're coming back.'

'Shouldn't you be making plans for uni?'

Who bloody cared? Ever since the debacle at Kallangur and the move back to Canberra I had been restless and dissatisfied. I had drifted from one short-term job to another. I felt homeless. I was homeless.

'It's just a holiday. Anyway, Eric needs to go.'

Eric did in fact have reasons to get away. Images of Elaine haunted him everywhere he went – at parties, at pubs, even when he hit a bit more smack, which no longer gave him the release he craved.

So I bought myself a backpack, a pup-tent, a hunting knife, a big Alvey sidecasting reel and a surf rod. Eric was spared the extravagance – he already had a bunch of camping gear stashed in his mum's garage – so he shouted us two ounces of best heads.

We set off in the big green Toyota wagon. Eric hammered the highway out through Yass, flouting the speed limit and overtaking cars and trucks three and four at a time.

'Hell, Eric! Slow down!'

'Live fast. Die young. Leave a good-looking corpse.'

'Prick. You didn't even make that up. Where d'you reckon we'll go?'

Eric said what we were both thinking. 'Who cares?'

As soon as I saw it, I knew it was too soon to be back at Kallangur. There were too many memories of Simone.

When we arrived Paul was at his new office. Mum was at another breeder's helping with a mating. Amy and Carole were at school. Apart from Hillary, the migrant girl from Manchester who Mum had hired for help around the kennels, Don was the only person home. He was in the old pioneer hut behind the main house, fixing up the floors and sealing the holes in the walls so he could use it as a bedroom and studio for his painting. He grunted a greeting as if we'd never been gone.

We scrounged up a couple of folding beds and cleared out the concrete-floored oven that had served as my room and still held a pile of dusty texts on anthropology. I knew more about the inside of a beer glass at the Royal Exchange than what was on the inside of *Man and Nature*.

Next morning Paul had us behind the wheel of the Kombi heading for the tip with a load of rolled-up newspapers covered in puppy-shit.

After that we were supplied with tools, concrete mix, and an assortment of timbers. We were instructed to build Paul a chicken shed.

Honestly we toiled, but the framework was unstable, untrue and downright dangerous. Don came to the rescue, expertly driving in nails and screws to save the structure from justified collapse.

We started on the roof. Heat vibrations shimmered mercilessly off the corrugated iron. Eric was sweating so much he looked like he'd just taken a shower in his clothes.

'This isn't how we planned our holiday.'

There was no argument from me. 'Let's head north. Tomorrow.'

Conversation at the dinner table that night was more than a little strained.

'What in heaven's name are you going to do with yourselves?' demanded Paul.

'I dunno. Live off the dole. That's what it's for.'

'You're not owed a living.'

'Well that's stiff, because I'm taking one.'

Later Mum suggested that she could send in applications for some journalism courses. She knew about the minor articles and book reviews I'd toyed with at the paper.

'I dunno, Mum.'

'Ian, these days that piece of paper is pretty important. You have to plan for the future some time.'

We left the next morning.

A bloke named Keith, who we knew from school, had rented a shack along a dirt road near Coolum Beach.

Tanned, indolent and semi-naked, Keith drank coffee, smoked home-grown dope and tripped on gold-topped mushrooms. We tried some too. I remember being terrified by an enormous spider with a vibrating multicoloured abdomen and a colossal web that blockaded the entire front verandah.

From Keith's place we went on up to Noosa, where we met some girls in the hippie-haven campgrounds at the end of the esplanade where the river met the sea.

I don't even remember the name of the girl Eric left me with, but she obviously liked the look of me.

'Let's fuck.'

I tried. I really did. But the body didn't feel right. It wasn't Simone.

Next day, with Eric and his girl gone to Granite Bay for skinny-dipping, I got drunk at the Noosa pub and scribbled a postcard.

Simone, I can't get you out of my mind. There's no one in the world for me but you. I'm applying for some courses. Mum will let me know. See you soon!

Love Ian

On New Year's Eve Keith from Coolum borrowed a flat close to the Noosa pub. The flat's big windows revealed a tropical tree scape – mango, pawpaw, and fragrant frangipani.

Not that we noticed. Eric and Keith brewed about thirty magic mushrooms into a ghastly treacly coffee. We gagged our way through the lot. Keith rolled a five-paper joint licked with opiated hash. A few minutes later I felt uncontrollably sick and rushed to the loo. But the hallucinogen was in my blood.

We found ourselves parked in a sandy cutting that led down to the wild sweep of surf-beach. Sunset bled through writing layers of cloud. We tumbled towards the water. The sand was sucking at my feet as I tried to follow the others. The sand was up to my knees. I was on my knees.

The waves roared at me, their faces flashing in the sun. I lost sight of Eric and Keith. The sun disappeared; the sand turned to ice. Desperate for something to warm me, I fled for the car and there I found my fishing knife. The blade glinted in the growing dark. It sang to me to sink it in, to find the warmth I craved. The peace.

I touched the point to the palm of my hand; there was a pinpoint of blood. I pushed and the blood increased.

My blood started singing to me. 'Be still,' it crooned, and my body calmed its shivering. 'Watch. Wait.'

I obeyed. I watched my blood as it bubbled and trickled and grew. I focused on it alone.

And suddenly the knife, the car, the screaming sea were gone, swallowed by my blood. I was watching from a void. Bloody clouds wreathed a new planet. There was nothing else but this planet. It hung in space, throbbing with the energy of all it had swallowed.

Then the planet exploded, yawning its wonders, hurling new stars and new worlds into the cosmos. I was a comet too close to the heat of the baby sun. My orbit slowed; I could see the earth. Billions of people circled endlessly, powerless, born and dead and born again, babes in arms sucking the milk of their own mortality, time-worn ancients with bones turned to dust, dragged down into the ever-drawing drain of death, emerging new and fresh only to face the drag again.

For the impossibility of infinity the people lived and hoped and cried and circled. After the end of time there came a dimness to their sphere and the people prayed that the universe was dying, that it would turn to darkness. To Nothing.

But there was no Nothing. There was a dormant babble: the billion voices of chaos humming like bees trapped in a jar. The cosmos yawned again. Worlds were made again. The people believed again in the possibilities of their lives.

I cried for this endless curse of life.

I dropped the knife. There was no point. It couldn't kill me. Nothing could kill me. Except whatever it was that controlled the Cosmic Yawn.

We went back to the pub. Eric bought some beers and a bottle of tequila. The place was packed with sun-tanned girls with opaque eyes and salty peroxides; big-shouldered surf-riders wearing lurid singlets; and families eating salads of beetroot and orange slices while the dads nursed another pot and perved on the nubile bra-less hippie girls.

I wanted to tell people about the Cosmic Yawn. They had to be warned. They were all being dragged towards it. They had to be warned!

I tried to convey my desperation to Eric. I explained the trap of the Yawn.

'Bummer trip! There's a party down the beach.' He waved the tequila. 'Let's go.'

In the morning I found Eric sprawled unconscious by the ashes of a beach bonfire, arm across a semi-clad maiden I'd never seen before. She would have made quite a spectacle once the tourists started strolling. I decided it would be wise to wake them.

The girl clutched an automatic hand to breast, then struggled to focus. By the time I could rouse Eric, she was long gone.

He sampled the sand sprinkling from his hair and spat. Then, with sudden energy, he was on his feet and jumping from a sandbank into the rushing tidal outflow of the Noosa River.

He shouted good morning. And as he was washed out to sea, he yelled with joy, 'Just another day in the Cosmic Yawn.'

We were on the move again. When Eric and I had reached Gladstone, a place we had more or less decided to make our base, we had taken one look at the dusty inhospitable streets and decided that there was no way we would seek the dole there.

We set off at sunrise, travelling down from Eungella through Mackay and back to the coast from Proserpine with only a pie for lunch and a packet of Drum. In a pub at Mackay we met a bloke who sold us a good deal of heads. Apart from a pineapple and half-a-dozen bananas, that was our total stash. Money was getting short.

We found some campgrounds scratched from forest a mile or so from the Shute Harbour wharf. A rusting EH wagon sat beneath a sprawling shade tree, drawn up to face a picnic bench and fireplace. Strung between the tree and a post was a rope festooned with Stubbies and sarongs worn thin by constant wear.

Eric and I watched as the campers returned to their site. The man was the colour of earth and ochre. His close-cropped hair was bleached by salt and sun. In one hand he carried a big hand-line, in the other a large red and white striped emperor fish. The woman wore a cotton-laced top and a sarong hitched to her hips. Like the man she was barefoot and deeply tanned. Her hair was swept back black and shining from the sea.

The couple gave us a brief inspection. I put up a hand of greeting and got a nonchalant wave from the man. The woman found a knife from the store of gear in the back of their car and sat down to prepare the fish.

The last time I'd seen a fish as nice as that emperor was when Eric had landed a fat writhing half-metre flathead a week or so back, on his first cast at Tannum Sands. We'd had inadequate cooking gear and had ruined the barbecue. But it didn't smell like the woman was going to stuff up her fish. There was a whiff on the wind of ginger and freshly cut lemongrass. Ravenous from the smell, we went about sorting our gear.

'You guys look like you could use a feed.'

She was gorgeous close up. There was a tiny butterfly tattoo on the topmost swell of her right breast. It fluttered as she breathed. Eric and I were both near-mute. I think we must have nodded.

'Well,' she said, 'how about we swap you a couple of those bananas for some scrummy red emperor.'

Eric agreed, then patted his shirt pocket and suggested,

with immense chivalry, 'Perhaps we can offer you a little smoke.'

The siren nodded graceful acceptance. We followed her over to the picnic bench.

Rachel was from Cap-de-la-Madeleine on the Saint Lawrence River, equidistant between Quebec and Montreal. Not that she seemed to care.

'What does it matter where I'm from? I'm here, now. That's the only thing that counts.'

She stretched to embrace the campgrounds as if they were all of tropical Queensland, the trees of the forest, the evening clouds that flared gold from the setting of the sun.

Rene was taciturn and self-contained. Apart from admitting he was a Kiwi he was disinclined to talk. Rachel told us that they had been camped at Shute for several weeks. Their car had broken down. Rene had ordered the part but couldn't pay for it until his dole came through. He looked like he could wait forever.

The fish was sweet and steamy. I was embarrassed by the way Eric and I tucked in. After dinner Rene rolled an enormous joint and offered the first blast to Eric.

Later, I wandered in the forest. The last of sunset faded orange on the trunks while huge thunderheads loomed in over the Whitsunday Islands to deliver the evening downpour. I was drenched in moments, but it was better than any shower. I took off my clothes and let myself be hammered, sluiced clean. The fat raindrops belted onto my upturned face. Even though she was nowhere to be seen, I found myself sharing quite perfectly Rachel's moment.

Rachel said if Eric and I chipped in to get some essential ingredients, she'd do the cooking and we could share the meals. Being the ones with wheels that worked, we'd take a weekly trip to Proserpine. On the first visit we put in for the dole and Rachel plundered the fruit and vegetable stalls. She bought flour and baked a big crusty damper in the fire.

Despite my fancy new gear, Rene and Eric caught all the fish. But I did manage to snare an angry giant of a crab. Rachel made a chilli dipping sauce befitting its fury, and we dipped its flesh with reverence.

Together we swam and sunned on the rocks around the big waterhole pounded out by constant cascade from the cliffs above. Butterflies, big and bright, dipped about on the forest fringe and there was an ongoing chatter of insects and birdsong. We washed our travel-grimed clothes and dried them on the rocks. They even looked ironed. We felt so clean and good.

Eric and I took a day trip over to South Moll Island to check out the resort and see if there was any casual work to be had. We were treated with suspicion and refused. We bought beers we couldn't afford and sat at a poolside table, hoping to watch lithe brown bodies, affronted instead by the pasty and imperfect. So we rattled off a few South Moll beach-and-sunshine postcards. One to Kallangur announcing our whereabouts. Another to Simone, saying I wished she was here. Fiscally marooned in the Whitsundays.

Every day we'd check in at the post office, increasingly desperate for the freedom of the dole cheque.

I received a telegram from Mum: PROVISIONALLY ACCEPTED CANBERRA COLLEGE. WRITING SAMPLES REQUIRED. DUE 28 JANUARY.

The deadline was just a week away. I had no time to lose. I had to choose. A dash to Kallangur to write like mad and meet the deadline, or this easy life in the campground with Rene, Rachel and Eric. Standing on the footpath outside the post office, the four of us debated my dilemma.

Except for four dollars and some loose coins I was broke. Eric was in no position to help; the Toyota was nearly out of petrol and he was as broke as me. Rene was still waiting for his dole payment, which meant ours was even further away. If I went, I was going alone.

'Stick around,' said Eric. 'If they'll accept you this time, they'll accept you next time.'

'Simone won't wait. You know she's hassling me to get my life organised.'

'This girl,' said Rene. 'If she likes you that much she'll let you do things in your own time.'

'Yeah, but I promised.'

'Follow your heart,' sang Rachel.

I didn't even wait until morning.

I lucked a ride to the Bruce Highway and another into Mackay. Trudging through town in the gathering dark I saw someone lurking beside the railway line. He waved at me to come over, his eyes bright with excitement.

'The train's due any minute. Jump a wagon, mate. Quicker than hitching.'

So when the train lumbered out of the yards, slowly gathering speed, I chased my way aboard an empty flatcar. I could hear the kid yelling, 'Good luck on the Marlborough stretch.' I didn't see him again.

As the train ferried me southwards, I rolled out my bag and jammed myself up against the rear bulwark of the car to keep from rolling overboard if I fell asleep.

Which I did, dreaming of a perfect day when I carried Simone's books into our rose garden, our love embodied by the scented down of perfumed petals.

I was caught at Saint Lawrence soon after midnight, when the train pulled up to take on freight. Someone shone a torch in my eyes.

'This is where you get off, sunshine.'

Beefy arms hauled at my sleeping bag, dragging my weight across the floor of the car. I barely had time to grab my pack. I was heaped on the platform by the station master who was wearing a grease-and-sweat-grimed blue shirt with epaulettes and a tarnished badge. He jerked a thumb into the humid gloom.

'Road's over there.'

There was a moon-white dusty road disappearing into the ugly low scrub that infested so much of this part of Queensland. It was barely a track. I hoped it led west to the Bruce Highway. God help me if it only snaked south to Marlborough, which was a good fifty miles away.

'Can I sleep in the waiting room until it gets light?'

'You can piss off quick, is what you can do.'

The Marlborough Stretch. People were murdered here. Their bodies were dumped among rocks and hidden by trees, undiscovered until the bones were bleached.

I sat by the road, waiting for the red dusty dawn and the chance for a ride. It came with a screech of cockatoos and the crunch of tyres on gravel from a farmer's ute. I stuck out my thumb. The car passed in a cloud of dust. I could just see the driver giving me the forks.

Nearing noon, with not another car gone past, I gave up hitching and lugged my pack back to the railway station. The station master was still there. I spent a precious dollar on a ticket to Marlborough and asked if it was okay to use the waiting room.

'Pay your fare, you can use the facilities.'

They were not much to boast of. The urinal vibrated with blowflies, and the stench was choking. Just before the train arrived, the station master offered me a smoke and said he was sorry that he had chucked me off the freight wagon.

'You've got to do your job, eh? You never know when some bastard from Brisbane might be watching.'

Back on the Bruce Highway outside Marlborough, I was offered a ride in a white Valiant. The car's interior was crammed with grubby rags of clothing, batteries, crushed beer cans, empty cigarette packets and hand-tools. It stank of beer and stale smoke.

The driver gunned us off down the road. 'Wanna beer?'

Did I bloody ever! But did I wanna die? No thanks. This bloke was pissed off his trolley. He had one hand on the wheel, the other wrapped around a beer. I clutched my own can and prayed.

Eventually, my benefactor's supply ran out and he vowed to find a pub before closing time. He stopped to stock up, wobbling back to the car with another dozen cans. I offered to drive. He didn't even ask if I knew how.

I by-passed Gladstone, and we were clear of Gin Gin and Childers before my companion stirred. We were about twenty kilometres south of his turn-off.

'Doesn't matter, son. Just pull up here. I'll do a uey and that'll be that.'

And so it was. Somewhere near Maryborough, I rolled out my bag on a grassy spot beneath a tree and slept. I awoke soaked by drenching dew under a clear blue sky. The day felt lucky. Even the prospect of Kallangur seemed good.

I jagged a ride immediately with a salesman type in a brand new Falcon. He stopped for breakfast at a bright new roadhouse in Gympie. When he found out how broke I was he bought me bacon, eggs, toast with lashings of butter and little packets of marmalade, and the best coffee I had ever tasted.

Eric, Rene and Rachel turned up at Kallangur two weeks later in Eric's Toyota, bearing dole cheques for all. The EH had been abandoned, and the back of the Toyota was crammed with gear.

'Do your exams?'

I nodded.

'Well, looks like your problem with Simone is solved.'

It wasn't. I was accepted at the CCAE but I didn't go.

Instead I was to spend the next twelve months at Dad's, observing Australian democracy's darkest year on a brand new television in a brand new house in Geelong West.

Dad's tour of duty in Thailand was over. He'd been offered a senior posting with the Victorian government in Melbourne, and had offered me a deal too good to refuse. He said that he would move to Geelong so he could live near his brother, and commute to work. I could live with him and study journalism at Deakin University with no money worries and the use of his car.

I asked Simone to come with me, but she would not leave Canberra again. She said she would visit for a weekend.

Eric, who had returned to Canberra with me, just shrugged as if to say, here we go again.

The house in Geelong was a dapper two-bedroom affair on Laira Street. It was an easy walk to the railway station and to the city campus, which was, for the time being, at the Gordon Institute of Technology. Dad bought me a bed, a desk and a typewriter, and went off to work.

Formal classes hadn't yet begun when Simone flew down for her promised visit.

She stepped out of the plane in a low-cut red and white dress, very fashionable with her long brown legs and beautifully shaped black hair.

'You look great!'

She gave me a look that indicated that I certainly didn't.

'I know, pretty grotty. Sorry.' My hair was still tousled after the race from bed to the airport, speeding along in the brand new Renault 12 with the wind ripping away my hang-over from the orientation dance the night before.

We drove to Bell's beach. The sea wind was up and the place was wild and beautiful. We wedged ourselves in the shelter of a sandstone downspout for warmth.

One look at Simone in this intimacy and I knew. 'You've come to say goodbye.'

She nodded and for a time seemed to be gathering the words. 'It's best for us both. But we had a good time together, didn't we?'

I blinked at the sudden tears. She took the back of my hand, tracing the veins with a finger.

'You'll find someone else in no time.'

Then she grabbed me and hugged my whole being, like she was trying to take me in and hold me there. She succeeded. When Simone went back aboard the plane, a bit of my core flew with her. She holds it still.

The Gordon Institute of Technology was a shabby work-house where ruddy and bucolic young men and women with elastic-sided boots and moleskin pants discovered the complexities of Textiles and Wool Technology. I knew no one and observed friendships and alliances from a cocoon of loneliness.

But it wasn't long into that autumn of 1975 before all the arts and humanities classes moved to the new Deakin

University campus out along the Colac Road at Waurne Ponds.

Mr Craddock, my literature tutor, was a short woolly man with sideburns and corduroys and a wine-dark nose. He had a fondness for talking in an absurd form of rhyme.

'e e cummings the punctuation king and Lear we find will be our subjects dear this session, this double day, poem and play.'

The class would flutter loose-leaf folders and clatter their Bics, wondering if Mr Craddock would ever say something they could understand.

During one particularly confusing lecture, the class was interrupted by a new arrival.

'Pardon me, is this where I learn to write?'

I twisted to examine this impudent new student. She moved to a seat beside me, flashing me a dazzling almond-eyed isn't-this-a-hoot-but-what-a-load-of-bullshit smile.

To Mr Craddock, 'Sorry I'm late. I'm Lindall Lasch. I just enrolled.'

'Welcome to the class,' said Mr Craddock with the look of a man who scents trouble. 'Are you familiar with e e cummings?'

Lindall settled, instantly relaxed.

'Yep.'

'Good. Perhaps you can offer some ideas on why the poet pays such scant attention to the conventions of capitals.'

'They're only words. So he's decided it's okay if he changes them to suit his purpose.'

Mr Craddock gathered for the fray.

'Only words! Heresy, Miss Lasch.'

'It's only heresy if in the first place you have dogma to create the conflict.'

The class, dimly recognising the whiff of insult, shifted nervously.

I read Eric's letter in the student lounge.

Ian
Yes, I know I owe you a letter. Things have been happening since you left. Mum landed a job at the University of New England so she sold our house and moved to Armidale. I said I'd pay her rent but she said I'd blow my dole on dope and she'd still be paying the new mortgage. So she's gone and left me broke. It's a bit of a hassle scrounging up the rent here where I ended up, but so far I've managed. It's a share house on the Kingston shops side of Telopea Park. There are some real freaks here. You'd approve. Or maybe you wouldn't. You've been getting straight lately. I'll see you soon.
    Eric

Just as I finished, Lindall Lasch came sashaying up to me, balancing her books with coffee and a salad roll.

'I knew we'd be friends as soon as I saw you.'

I moved my stuff out of the way and she sat down. Long brown hair fell over her shoulders.

'What else do you know?' I asked her.

The corners of her lips were curled in permanent amusement.

'Your name's Ian. You're a Cancerian. You're turning

twenty. You're studying journalism and suchlike. You're a good writer.'

I was dumbfounded. She gave a playful push at my shoulder and hooted with laughter.

'Got you! I asked Mr Craddock. What do you know about me?'

'I just met you.'

'Come on. You can do better than that.'

'Your name's Lindall Lasch. I'd say you're twenty-two, twenty-three . . .'

'Boring.'

'That crack about dogma. Mr Craddock thinks he's going to have his hands full with you and he'll mark you like a bastard.'

'What else?'

'I like you. I like your eyes. How's that?'

She seemed pleased.

I gave Lindall a ride home in Dad's Renault. She was extremely talkative.

'Everyone seems to do arts, don't they? Boasting they're writing the Great Australian Novel. Secretly dreading they'll end up a teacher or a public servant living in the suburbs with a mortgage and a garden, making babies so the babies can do the same. I don't think I could stand being a teacher, but I think it's in my karma.'

'What kind of teacher?'

'Little kids,' she said. 'Still wide-eyed at all of life's marvels and mysteries. Open to all its possibilities. Before they get corrupted.'

Her house was along a terrace row that overlooked the

twinkle of shipping on Corio Bay. There was a spring-sprung couch on the porch, booming music from the end of a long corridor; warm lights and a smell of onions and garlic sautéing in a pan. A big kitchen table held candlesticks and a flagon of Seppelts red, a mulling bowl and matches.

Lindall introduced me to her house-mate Trish, who was cooking up something on the stove. Trish waved a casual hi.

Then I was ushered to Lindall's room. A double bed, covered by an intricate multi-panelled quilt, was set against the only window. A faded Oriental rug and a pile of big cushions rested in front of an iron-framed fireplace set with paper and kindling.

I continued my exploration as Lindall lit the fire. There was a panoply of miniature copper Asian gods on the mantle-piece. Above the gods hung a tapestry of a mandala blazing with colour. On another wall there was a desk and portable typewriter surrounded by books and notes.

Lindall selected a record from her large collection and worked the needle on the player until she found the place she wanted. She started to sing along.

'My favourite. Songs of love beat songs of hate every time.'

At dinner we were joined by the couple of the house – Geoff, tall and gaunt with long dark hair tied tight, the guru of this house on the hill; and Vikki, calm and generous with nun-like benevolence.

'So, you've decided to chase that little piece of paper,' said Geoff.

'It's something to do.'

'Ah, the no-harm-in-it theory! Don't you have any ambitions? Change the world? Rechart the course of history?'

'Fat chance of that.'

'Think global, act local?'

What was this idiot talking about?

'Right now I'm just happy living in the moment.'

Which came out sounding like another one of Jack Winters' warcries.

Ian

I'm living over in Reid, note the new address. I guess I fell too far behind on my rent for the taste of my previous housemates. C'est la guerre. *Can you loan me a hundred bucks? I wouldn't ask but I'm in a hole waiting for a guy to pay me back on a deal.*

Eric

Lindall and I went to see *Jesus Christ Superstar* starring Marcia Hines and Jon English at the St Kilda town hall. The performance started Lindall off on another one of her serious conversations.

'Do you believe in God?'

'No,' I replied.

'Fate?'

'No. Life is pointless chaos. It happens by accident.'

She thought about that for a while.

'I don't mean the God of Protestantism or Catholicism or the Koran or the Upanishads. That stuff's an invention by powermongers trying to keep ordinary people under control. Fear of divine vengeance and all that. I'm thinking about something else, bigger. An essential force.'

I told her about the night of the Cosmic Yawn, and agreed that there was definitely an energy. 'But why? Endlessly being bloody reincarnated. What for? Like you said: make babies and have mortgages. There has to be more to it all than that.'

Lindall gave me a look of sympathy.

'You sound so angry. Didn't you say the other night you want to live in the now?'

'Yeah.'

'Well, if you fuss and fume and say what's the point all the time, how can you? It's like that Buddhist thing about life is suffering. How maudlin! Every day is a gift.' She reached out and punched my arm. 'What say we wag tomorrow and go walking in the Otways.'

So we did. The colossal trees provided canopy cover for the skitter of animals and birds. Lindall wandered aimlessly, pointing out little things like the magical curl of tiny new fern leaves, chattering happily about her discoveries, totally in tune with the surrounds.

I struggled with words to tell the day in a poem. Next day, Lindall read it in silence. Her smile was gone.

'It's lovely, Ian. Thank you. I just wish I didn't have the feeling that I'm going to disappoint you.'

Ian
This Lindall of yours sounds a pretty fair sort. How soon they forget! Speaking of Simone, I saw her in Civic the other day on the arm of some bloke. He looked rich. Quite the dasher. C'est la guerre. Sorry about the delay with your money. I was ripped off.
    Eric

I was alarmed when Lindall went on a date with one of our classmates, a local lad named Steve. They went to a wool-shed dance near Anakie. Uninvited, I gatecrashed anyway. I got drunk and begged a ride home with them. Steve didn't look too thrilled.

'Oh, let him come,' said Lindall. Steve acceded with about as much warmth as the shiver-cold clear night. I couldn't have cared less.

'It's the new Ice Age,' I proclaimed, burrowing my face deep into the warm cradle of Lindall's shoulder so her hair fell all about me.

'Poor thing,' she laughed. 'You're freezing!'

She wrapped me in her arms and my happiness was complete.

Ian
It's going to be a while before you get your money. Sorry, but I've had some shit with the law. Busted holding a bag of dope and my needle. Anyway, I copped a $500 fine and they've given me a month to pay. My bloody mother refuses to help. Can't say I blame her really, but consider this: now I'll have to do some dealing to raise the cash. Not exactly what the court system had in mind . . .
    Eric

Lindall dated Steve again and I discovered the red delirium of jealousy. It shone through as Lindall and I sprawled among the cushions in front of her fire. The flames crackled merrily and occasionally spat as we worked on our notes.

'Do you love me?' she asked me.

I'd tried to say it with my poem. The vengeful bile rose inside me.

'I don't think I know what love is.'

Lindall gave me a deflated look. Then she realised what was going on.

'You're jealous! Oh, Ian, please don't be.'

I said nothing.

'You know what? You spend too much time inside that silly skull of yours. What is love? Analyse and dissect. Fifty points for each, like it's all an exam.'

When I left she gave me a kiss.

'Well, I love you. And your eyes are pretty when you're looking inside yourself.'

Lindall had another admirer. His name was Ed, a teacher-to-be studying his degree by day and heading for the surf at Torquay every free weekend. He was a mild-mannered, uncomplicated guy who loved to tell Lindall about the peace and power he found in his waves.

Ed, Trish and Lindall had been hoarding pay from part-time jobs, saving for a trip to Asia at the end of the year. I had no huge desire to travel once more to Asia, but I couldn't let Lindall go off alone. I decided to bludge the money off Dad.

But then I ruined everything. One night Ed and Steve rolled up to Lindall's to pay their usual evening respects with a flagon of Seppelts and a half-dozen bottles of draught. I was already in the kitchen, mulling up some dope for one of Trish's trademark five-paper joints. Lindall found some Steely Dan and turned up the volume. Geoff and Vikki smoked some weed with us, but he refused the wine and after a while went back to his meditations. Vikki got tipsy and made Ed dance with her.

Steve grabbed his chance and had Lindall on her feet. He sent a self-satisfied leer over her shoulder at me. I would have sulked, but Trish hauled me to my feet and we all danced and drank and smoked and drank and danced. I cut in on Steve a dozen times and was having a terrific time until I looked around sometime near midnight and noticed that Trish and I were alone. In her bedroom. She'd steered me there, and she wouldn't let me go.

'Where's Lindall?'

'She's with Steve. Leave them be.'

In my mind I was loving Lindall.

When I left, with the rain rattling on the roof, I saw that Lindall's light was on and she was reading. I couldn't help myself. I knocked and went in.

'I thought you were with Steve.'

Lindall gave a snort of disgust. 'So you thought you'd have a bit of revenge.'

I knew I was in strife, but I said it anyway. 'So you didn't . . .?'

'So what if we did? That's my business and it's fucking well none of yours.'

'Oh, shit . . .'

I made a move towards her, but she turned away.

'Go home, Ian.'

And I didn't understand that it was too late to tell her yes.

The opium den on Penang had become my haven. It was little more than a lean-to attached to the corrugated-iron hut where the Professor's wife ran the household business, squatting comfortably beside her brazier and cooking-pots, calmly fending off the nosy chickens and ducks roaming her porch.

The Professor knew me by sight. He ushered me into the dark square room that had reclining benches and wooden pillows. He took a packet of black-brown raw opium wrapped in banana leaf, divided it into four equal parts, and prepared my first pipe for the day. It was mid-morning.

With his white wispy beard and timeless eyes, the Professor looked a venerable philosopher. The reality, according to the legends of the Hippie Trail, was that he'd been a soldier in Chiang Kai Shek's Kuomintang and had fled Mao's revolution by vanishing on the Burmese side of the Golden Triangle. He had supposedly travelled down through the Thai hill country, eventually setting up this illicit business here in the fishing village of Telok Bahang, not far from George Town on the Malaysian island of Penang.

Though there were none at this hour, I'd come to know my fellow customers. Most were Chinese ancients like the Professor. They would chatter contentedly in the twilight of the den as they smoked. Other customers included Malays who were seeking relief from bodily aches and illnesses, and hippies like me – young, unkempt and clad in a motley mix of Western and Asian styles.

The pipe gurgled with mellow practice, resin bubbling at the flame as it transformed itself into the smoke flowing inside me. I relaxed, head on one of the wooden pillows, one leg propped against an upraised knee in the fashion of the den. The Professor made a second pipe. After the fourth I was nearly asleep and, for now at least, out of pain.

I stepped out along Telok Bahang's main street, blinking in the sunshine. In a shanty across from the police station an Indian woman sold fish curries. I would throw up if I ate. I walked past a big restaurant where old men gambled at Mah Jong and hippies sat vacantly waiting to take the bus to George Town. Heroin dealers sat alongside them, trying to strike a deal.

As usual, I ended up on the beach. The sand was fouled by years of flotsam from the fishing boats, but it was warm in the sun. This was where I had sat with Lindall, Trish and Ed only a month before. I spread my sarong and lazed there nodding off, temporarily forgetting everything that had gone before.

We'd just arrived. Telok Bahang was our first stop after the plane to Kuala Lumpur, a night train to Butterworth, and a dawn ferry to George Town where we had breakfasted on incomprehensible Chinese mysteries.

When we found out about the den we had a silly time sampling the Professor's product, then came down to the beach to sit at sunset. Ed and Lindall made jokes about opium dreams, Trish giggled guiltily at being so stoned, and I lay in a peaceful daze, unjustifiably warm with optimism.

Lindall roomed with Ed. For a week the Professor's pipes erased my envy. When the time came to move on the four of us shared a hotel room in Butterworth. Lindall dumped her pack on one of the double beds and left the rest of us to sort ourselves out while she negotiated a morning ride to Haadyai.

I commandeered the space beside Lindall. Ed shrugged and made nothing of it. When Lindall saw what I'd done she held her silence but, until she got sick of my insinuating little touches and gave me an angry hand-job, she ignored me.

I hated myself so much I could have died.

Haadyai was crawling with soldiers, on the alert because of some Muslim insurgency. I barely noticed. At the railway station, urchins tried to sell us mandarins and peanut brittle. On the train, Buddhist monks in saffron robes watched soldiers eye off the girls and give each other sly nudges. I drank Mekong whisky *nam* in the restaurant car and hoped the luxury of *kao pad* with tomato ketchup and a runny fried egg on top would make me feel better. It didn't. The train passed impossible crags exploding vertically from the sea of paddies, and waterways festooned with fish-nets.

We caught the hydrofoil to Koh Samui, a village fringed by palm plantations. I predicted with an accurate gloom-laden certainty that Lindall would say, 'I think everyone would be happier if us girls roomed together.'

Next day Lindall asked me to go to a local waterfall with her so we could talk. She walked so purposefully it was a struggle to keep pace.

'What's up?'

'Wait until we get to the waterfall.'

Trucks loaded with coconuts rumbled past. The labourers perched on top of the cargo, their faces wrapped in rags but still burned black by sun. We passed little groves where bandy-legged men urged willing monkeys into the arching palms. For once I was watching, and Lindall ignored it all. At the waterfall she took a brisk swim and as she finished towelling she started talking.

'There's no easy way to say this, so I'm not going to try. You're sapping all my energy. Right now I want my energy for myself. When we leave this place, I'm going up to Chiangmai. I'm going alone.'

Well, that was the end of the party. Ed said he wanted to go to Phuket. Trish went to Bangkok with Lindall but immediately flew home. I fled back to the Professor.

I was staying at a guest-house set behind a house owned by one of Telok Bahang's wealthy Chinese families. The guest-house had five sleeping rooms and a middle room with a table and chairs. Everything was made of unpainted wood. Apart from a faded map of Penang and a small red-and-gold shrine with an incense pot there were no decorations. The sleeping rooms had raised wall-to-wall platforms to stretch out on, the only cushioning a couple of roll-out mats. The bathroom stall consisted of a big tub of cold water and a dipper. Soap had to be kept inside a plastic container at night or the rats would eat it. The water fell through the slatted floorboards to the muddy tidal wash below. At low tide the mudskippers would come out to forage.

Most of the guests stayed only a few nights, but there was one other regular, a Canadian named Sam. Tangled and filthy, he too was a junkie. I offered him a joint I'd bought from a dealer on the bus after I had renewed my visa in George Town. It was laced with heroin. His hands shook violently as he accepted the joint, and I had to help him light it. But when the smack took over he was okay.

'Man, you're a life saver.'

He had a ball of pure white heroin tied tight in a condom. He refused to use it, because he was planning to ram it up his bum when he went home to Vancouver and sell it to finance his next trip overseas.

To save money, I ate and drank almost nothing. I owed rent to the guest-house. I had a tropical ulcer on my cheek, which oozed without stop. I'd reached the point where smoking opium for the sense of peace and ease was pointless, because it didn't come. I was smoking it because I needed it. I needed it so my guts would stop hurting.

One day I was leaving the Professor's when I saw a man through a restaurant window. He was sitting behind the old men playing Mah Jong, rigid in his chair. He had a dreadful look in his eye as he stared out at the street, but his focus was inward. I could tell he was horrified by what he saw.

Then he tipped over and died.

A fuss of people gathered where he'd fallen to the floor like a shrunken foetus. His skeletal left arm flopped free on the floor. I could see the needle tracks. A policeman rummaged through the dead man's papers and announced that his name was Marcel.

That night my ulcer burst in a flood of puss and blood. I mopped the wound with toilet paper and wept.

Early next day I packed up, paid the rent and left. The opium dream was over but the nightmare wasn't.

Too broke to pay for a train to Kuala Lumpur, I had to settle for a bus. It was full of a jouncing rabble of Malays, Indians, Chinese, caterwauling chickens in cages, baskets of evil-smelling durians, and children with runny noses.

The bus belched into the crowded terminus just on sunset. I found a phone and called the airline, saying I was ready to return to Melbourne. I was told that the next plane was in two days. Head splitting, belly rumbling with famine, I hoisted my pack and set off to find a cheap hotel. There weren't any, but my luck was in. I'd found a likely place and was whingeing that the tariff was too high when I heard an Australian voice behind me.

'You wanna share my room, mate? Split the cost.'

That's how I met Ray. He was about my age, with a thick well-groomed blond beard and eyes that seemed to find amusement in everything. He was from Hobart and, as coincidence always has it, he was flying home on the same plane as me. But first, he explained, he needed my help.

'What for?'

'You'd better come up to the room. I'll show you.'

The room had proper beds and a chest of drawers. Ray fished in one of the drawers and pulled out a plastic shopping bag full of heads.

'We have to smoke all this before we catch the plane.'

I smiled for the first time in weeks. Ray opened the shutters and soon the oil and diesel fumes from the traffic outside mixed with the aroma of burning hemp.

The next two days passed painlessly. Ray had plenty of money. He gave me some antiseptic ointment. He shouted me to a movie in a fancy new shopping plaza. We found a Western-style burger bar glaring with fluorescent cleanliness and gorged on a feast of hot dogs, hamburgers and root-beer. The taxi driver who took us to the airport would have been stoned by the mere smell of us. We insinuated ourselves onto the upstairs flight lounge of the Jumbo and guzzled great gratis draughts of beer and claret, going home under the tolerant eye of the stewards.

Sobriety struck at Tullamarine Airport. Ray was making his connection for Hobart, my oasis dried up. The first challenge was getting back to Geelong. I called Dad's office. He was in a meeting but his secretary said she'd arrange ten dollars if I could pick it up, so I shuttled into the city, collected the money and walked to Swanston Street to take the train home.

By the time Dad got home I'd had my first hot shower for months and was parked in front of the gas heater trying to fathom the television news. I could tell he was worried by my appearance. My ulcer wound still gaped and I knew I was too thin. He wanted me to tell him about the trip and whether I'd be resuming at Deakin.

That night I dreamed of Lindall tanning on a beach in Thailand. When I tried to touch her she snarled at me and said it was time to get a life of my own. I woke in a sweat and knew I couldn't go back to uni.

I went to the Commonwealth centre to register for the dole, but Malcolm Fraser's new government in Canberra had pledged an end to bludging. I was given a train ticket to Mildura. I was to earn a living picking grapes, and I was to leave that night. I hadn't even unpacked.

Dad bought some huge T-bones for a farewell feast and drove me to the station, stress and care worn in his eyes.

'Are you sure this is wise?'

'No.'

'Then why go?'

'I dunno. I just have to.'

The government didn't stretch to sleepers. I found myself in a compartment with five other men, all bound for the sultana blocks of Mildura. They carried wretched gladstone bags clinking with bottles of cheap port. The compartment stank of tobacco and body odour.

The train rattled out of the dusk and into the night. I climbed into the luggage rack and, using my pack for a pillow, tried to sleep. But sleep wouldn't come. I kept having flashes of the Professor's den and cravings for the contents of his soothing pipe. My belly swilled about with the rolling of the carriage.

I started hallucinating. The train would never stop; these men were my companions forever. They leered up at me with gappy smiles. I sat up with a start and smashed my head against the carriage roof. My stomach heaved.

I hurled myself to the floor and threw open the compartment door, running down the corridor towards the toilet.

I didn't make it. The vomit was backing up into my

mouth. I found the carriage exit door and dragged it open, almost sucked outside by the sudden rush of air. I grabbed a hand-grip and held on as I hurled my guts into the night.

It was getting light by the time I stopped vomiting. Even the bile was gone.

The train stopped at Red Cliffs and unloaded some of the pickers-to-be. I watched as they were casually pointed at in groups of four and five and herded into the back of farmers' utes.

The same fate awaited me in Mildura. Our farmer was a monosyllabic Italian. He told us the rules as we drove into town. We'd work from seven until five with an hour for lunch if we wanted to stop. We cooked and kept for ourselves. We'd be paid by the basket of picked fruit. More work, more money. He stopped at a grocery shop and told us to buy ourselves some food. I selected some biscuits, some baked beans, a loaf of bread and three chocolate bars. I ate some of the candy as we left town, heading for the block.

The sun was getting high. Heat mirages shimmered on the road at the top of each rise. Rows of vines bulged in every direction, their colours bleached by the sun. Gaggles of pickers sweated and burned.

We unloaded in front of a greasy fly-blown kitchen and a windowless dormitory filled with iron beds with sagging springs and naked stained mattresses. As it dawned on me that this slum was to be my home until the end of the picking season, my stomach heaved again. I ran outside and voided the chocolate.

Then I hefted my pack, told the farmer he could pick his own grapes, and started back towards town.

I spent the next three days huddled inside my pup-tent in a campground beside the River Murray. I slept most of the time, twisting under the weight of strange disturbing dreams, venturing out only to use the toilet and to vomit the bile of my addiction and my loss.

Gradually I got the opium out of my system. I sampled some biscuits. On the third night I ate baked beans on toast cooked over a fire I made myself. I took a shower. While I was drying my hair I took a look at myself in the mirror. I was pretty gaunt, but the welt on my cheek was almost healed. My eyes were clear, and there was a look in them I hadn't seen before. It reminded me of the dead Marcel's staring eyes, and the shadows and creases that had wrinkled the window to his soul.

Seeing that look, I knew I was lucky that I'd lived to notice it.

While I was drying out on the river, Dad received important news. He sent me money for a ticket back to Geelong. On the way home to Laira Street he explained that he had been offered the top job in the New South Wales archives.

The implications were clear. If I wanted Dad's company, I'd be moving to Sydney.

'You know if you want to stay on at Deakin I'll support you, but I'll have to sell the house.'

'Dad, I'm not going back.'

'For God's sake, you came third in the class!'

'I'm not going back. I'd be wasting my time.'

'What about coming up to Sydney, then? Transfer your credits.'

'I can't do that either.'

'Why?'

'I want to write.'

'Do it in Sydney.'

'I want to be close to Lindall.'

So, while Dad tidied his affairs once more, I rented the front room in a pioneer cottage near Bannockburn on the road from Geelong to Ballarat. Dad's removalists delivered my desk and typewriter then continued north to Sydney. He stopped in with a bottle of champagne to wish me luck.

'I know you've got some feelings you want to try and sort out. I just hope you don't find out it's all too turbulent to tell. If you want to talk, you know where to find me.'

And for the first time in years he gave me a hug. He squeezed me tightly, almost as if he wanted to plant inside me a little of the wisdom he'd gathered along his own path of losses and loves gone wrong.

The back half of the Bannockburn house was occupied by a landscape painter named Provis. Provis looked like a Canadian lumberjack with his flannel shirts and four-day stubbles, but he was as bent as an s-hook. He had a boyfriend named Alex who was studying in the university library. This gave Provis the chance to nip into Geelong and hop on the Melbourne train for a quick visit to his favourite sauna. He'd be back in time for dinner, which Alex would make while Provis swore and fussed at his painting as if he'd just contended with a dreadful day of creative frustrations and was doing well to keep the lid on his temper. On days when Alex had few classes and the Melbourne run wasn't on, Provis had the flagon out and was three-parts pissed by lunch time.

One such day, Provis tried to plant a kiss on me. I told him to fuck off or I'd flatten him, but this merely served to enhance my status as an object of his lust. I'd be in my room, tapping uninspired on the inanimate Olivetti, and Provis would be in the kitchen with his easel and the omnipresent odour of linseed, bellowing operatic arias interspersed with falsetto chirrupings such as, 'Can you hear me?' and, 'Are you ready yet, darling?'

I could bear only so much of this before I would escape on the rusty pushbike that came with the rent and cycle the several kilometres into Bannockburn. There I would check at the post office, hoping my dole cheque had turned up. If I had sufficient funds I would hit the live-music pint-glass pubs in Geelong and, thus fortified, turn up at Lindall's to be there in person while she ignored my mute entreaties to let things be the way they were before I fucked everything up.

And then I'd cycle back to the cottage, where the pages stared at me, terribly blank. I in turn would stare out at the traffic humming by on the Ballarat highway, yearning for the freedom of the road, and scared shitless of the future.

Provis threw a big party for all his gay mates from Melbourne. There was a long snaking queue along the road from Geelong. The cottage writhed with drag queens and muscle men decked in leather. Provis introduced me as the only straight in the place. 'But,' he added, leering, 'a straight with promise.'

I found one of the few girls there. She said she was a lesbian, and she withered at my attentions. I got her drunk and took her to bed anyway to sate my loneliness.

In the morning I discovered that someone had used my 'manuscript' – a few pathetic pages – to soak up vomit. Also floating in the putrid pool was the letter I'd just received from Eric.

Ian
Life is fucked. I lost my licence. First they picked me up for speeding. No big deal, a fine, but then they got me for being drunk. Another fine, but still, alas, the least of my worries. I copped a case of hepatitis despite my precautions, and now I feel like a bag of shit. C'est la guerre. *Somehow I have to dry out.*
Eric

Eric. Still the only friend I could count on.

I hurled the fouled pages of my writer's pretence into the yard. Then I stuffed a bunch of clothes into my bag and was gone without a word to anyone.

Back in the bar at ANU students' union I realised how much everything had changed in Canberra. The jugs of flat brown beer, the ash-grey smoke haze, the belt and throb of the juke box, the ugly bessa-block walls festooned with graffiti – these were the same as ever. But I saw few faces I recognised from the days of my own debaucheries there, and the people I did know treated me as a visitor. Eric was making deals with people I'd never met. I'd become a stranger in my own town.

Eric's connections were people who rarely saw the sun. They were pale and big-eyed from nocturnal creepings among the dope-dealing safe-houses that sustained them, their shirts long-sleeved to hide the needle tracks, their hair a draggle of indifference and neglect. These people sold my friend the substance that enslaved him.

Tall and spindly, Eric looked as if he was about to tip over. His translucent skin stretched across withered sinew. His eyes were dead.

One night we were invited out to a sharehouse where a girl we'd known in school was raising a child among paint-peeled walls and unwashed dishes gathering flies in a rancid kitchen. The lounge room had an expensive hi-fi that was playing Pink Floyd's 'Dark Side of the Moon'. There was a ritual sharing of the needle and spoon. The sight of Eric tightening a belt over his bicep to stand the vein out hard for the needle and rush was too much to endure. I crashed out of the house, gasping for clean air. The stars watched, hanging in the ether with their impersonal bright glimmering magic, untouched by the human decay below.

I walked for hours, towards the centre of my night-silent Canberra. Down by the lake, I threw rocks at the water. The ripples rolled back to mock me, just as they had when Simone had dumped me. This city had become so lonely, now that its public buildings no longer served me.

Next day I urged Eric to go north with me again. He

made excuses about having no wheels and no money. If I was going, I was going alone.

Farewell Lake George with its fences disappearing in orderly lines to the middle of its waters. Farewell bushranger Ben Hall, dead at Collector. Hello once more to that roadside waiting place outside Goulburn. I stood in the rain as the cars shooshed by, their drivers oblivious to the drizzle in my eyes as I wished that Eric was there to share the emptiness of my heart.

Dad had found himself a unit in Lane Cove, not far from the roaring Pacific Highway.

His face lit up at the sight of the miserable prodigal at the doorstep and he made me welcome once more. In a week or so, my belongings were retrieved from Bannockburn and I was established comfortably in the spare room. I was free to come and go as I pleased, which I did, not even bothering to claim the dole, obliviously taking advantage of the unconditional support offered by this good man who still loved me.

I found *Siddhartha*, the book for 'seekers', among the rest of my books and read it in a single sitting. The ending – Siddhartha calmly watching the endless reincarnated flow of humanity drifting past in the great river of life – put a more comforting construction on the terrors of the Cosmic Yawn, and it helped me hatch a plan.

When Dad came home that night, I happily ate his chops and sausages and mashed potatoes and kippers and talked of a beggar's life on the road.

'A beggar!'

'Yeah. Like a wandering *saddhu* in search of enlightenment.'

'First a writer, now a what d'you call it! For Christ's sake, why not knuckle down and get a bloody degree?'

'Dad, you're starting to sound like Paul.'

If there was one thing likely to insult my Dad, it was that. But he held his tongue and refrained from making further judgements. And he didn't say what perhaps he wanted to say most of all: 'Don't go away again and leave me lonely.'

I huddled under the bus shelter near the Gore Hill TV towers, trying to avoid the sudden Sydney downpour. A bus pulled up and unloaded a cascade of commuters. The last to get off, a crouched figure tottering down the steps, blinked his eyes into mine.

'Eric!'

He gave me his crooked smile.

'I decided you needed someone to look after you. That is, if you're still interested in going north again.'

This time I recognised the mist in my father's eyes when we said goodbye.

We decided to head up to Kallangur where we would have free rent and a regular supply of the neighbouring dairy farmer's magic mushrooms.

When we arrived, Amy told us about a couple of bed-rooms just vacated in a sharehouse at Auchenflower. Now studying social work at St Lucia, Amy lived there herself. Rent was only fifteen bucks a week, food kitty about the same.

The weatherboard house was enormous, with six bed-rooms. The back of the house rested on typical Queensland stilts as the land tipped away towards the Brisbane River. There were broad steps out the front which made a good viewing area for sunsets.

Besides Amy, there were three other girls in the house. Christine was in the matronly class, lively and witty but inclined to be the one to make sure we did our share of cleaning and that I regularly contributed my only dish to the huge dinner table in the even huger lounge room. This fare consisted of a mash of zucchinis, bananas and cheese. I'd learned the recipe from Lindall, who had gleaned it from one of those Hare Krishna cook books they flog on street corners.

Eric was impressed with the freckled, green-eyed, red-haired Marion. She sang at the Folk Club in town, and she'd dance at the drop of a hat with a wild Celtic aura.

Then there was Julie, dark-eyed, dark-haired, perfect white complexion, serious-minded and polite. She was studying to be a vet and, like Dad, was also a bit of a thes-pian. Julie was always off auditioning and as often as not landing the part.

There was something vaguely Camelot about the Auchenflower house. The place was a magnet for visitors. There were countless impromptu parties. The big table hosted numerous noisy debates, most of the time with someone lying on its surface, too drunk to stand. We had no Arthurs or Merlins or Lancelots, but there were plenty of jokers and minstrels.

My brother Don and his sculptor mate Johnno were regular visitors. They would arrive with guitar and flagon respectively and while Don tuned up, Johnno would hand out brimming glasses. We'd all get pissed singing 'Goodnight Irene' and 'Me and Bobby McGhee'. When we ran out of wine we'd rabble down to the pub and buy some more, or stay there drinking pot after pot and watching the girls. We would invariably collect more visitors and vagrants to trip over on the lounge-room floor in the hungover morning. A cup of coffee and a joint, a record whacked on the stereo, and the party would start again. If freedom meant having no responsibility to anyone but yourself, Eric and I had it made.

Much to Eric's amusement, the spirit of the wandering *saddhu* had stayed with me.

I meditated and practiced yoga and read *Zen and the Art of Motorcycle Maintenance*. I began to regard myself as an expert in matters mystical and expounded my theories to anyone who'd listen. This consisted of nobody except an Indian kid who lived with his parents in a flat next door. His name was Govind but he told me his name was Jesus.

Govind came to visit me frequently to discuss our universal mutual Jesusness until one night there was a commotion in his flat. I tipped out of bed quickly enough to see Govind struggling in the arms of burly men who were bundling him into the back of an ambulance. He was screaming my name for help.

In the morning Amy confronted me.

'What kind of shit have you been putting into his head? He's a schizophrenic!'

Some fucking messiah. Siddhartha of the seventies.

Om.

According to the rules of *saddhu*-hood, earthly desires are supposed to be existential fripperies soared beyond by the ego-free cosmic consciousness of simply Being.

But the sight of Julie gave me a boner. My sleep was disturbed by humid visions.

The Brisbane night-life scene was definitely not the place to seek relief. For starters, it was dangerous. Half the girls you would ask to dance would have boyfriends the size of Mal Meninga. The rest were usually drag queens. Secondly, the temptations were just too many and too frustrating.

One night, Eric, Amy and I went to a pub where a country-rock outfit called Dave Dood and the Country Characters was packing in the punters.

The girl taking the money was downright gorgeous. She had lush cascading curls of strawberry blonde hair, and dark sardonic eyes. Her smile to welcome the customers had a hint of disdain, which drove me nuts because I immediately wanted to be the one who'd win the genuine article. She had a long, elegant neck wrapped in a neat kerchief, cowgirl style; a denim shirt open to the top of small pert breasts;

long-leg Levis covering shapely hips; and fancy-tooled leather boots with pointy toes and heels. Amy and Eric were talking to this girl. They knew her!

'And this is my brother Ian,' said Amy. 'Ian, meet Toni.'

'Hi,' I said, delivering one of the most original introductory lines of modern times. Inexplicably undevastated, she took my money.

'Hope you like the show,' she said in an American accent.

I didn't pay the band any attention that night. As soon as we sat down and ordered drinks I started craning my neck to see the girl by the door.

'Who is she?' I demanded.

'Don't get your hopes up,' advised Eric. 'She goes with the drummer.'

After that I became a Dave Dood devotee. Not that it did me any good. The drummer knew his way around a kit and the bastard could sing a bit too. He had a song about a grandpa who had a wandering eye. To my despair, Toni didn't.

'Forget it,' said Eric. 'Try closer to home.'

So the next time Julie auditioned I went along and tried out for a chorus part in an amateur production of *Joseph and his Amazing Technicolour Dreamcoat*.

One night after late rehearsals we made coffee and Julie put Bob Dylan on in her bedroom. If dogs run free, then why not we? It seemed to me the invitation was plain.

'Ian, I have a boyfriend!'

'But he's in Toowoomba. I'm here.'

'Not for long!'

She swung me to my feet and revved me effortlessly out of her bedroom as if I were a newly vaccinated poddy calf.

'I don't know what to do about you,' said Paul.

'You don't have to do anything,' I said. 'It's my life.'

'Which – like Eric – you are completely wasting.'

I was ready for this one, and for once I had a come-back that would silence the critic. Eric and I had been forced by the Department of Social Security to learn a trade, so we had both taken the Commonwealth Public Service exams.

'No I'm not. I'm joining the public service. Department of Veterans Affairs. Starting Monday.'

'Well, hallelujah!' Paul saluted me with his glass, then changed the subject.

'Have you spoken to Eric about those vials of morphine that went missing from my glove box?'

'He says he had nothing to do with it.'

'Bloody liar. I should have him charged.'

'Maybe you just misplaced them.'

'I've looked. Ian, he stole those drugs. You and Amy are living with a criminal. You should kick him out.'

'Paul, Eric's my best mate. He needs help. Abandon him and he'll just slide even further downhill.'

'Let him slide. He's only going to take you with him.'

'I can't. It wouldn't be fair.'

'Why? What's he ever done for you?'

'He's stuck by me. He's always done that. I have to do the same.'

All the old diggers were coming north to die. This was the result of good weather and Gerrymander Joh's policy that nobody should have their final act on earth encumbered by taxes.

I was P28, the busiest Transfers Clerk in the entire commonwealth. It was my task to load the new arrivals into Brisbane's umbilical computer system and ensure they exited the one they were sent their money from before. A good number of pensioners would turn up at the counter wanting to know what had happened to their payments and I'd find out that some idiot from Melbourne or Adelaide had forgotten to forward their files. I'd get on the phone and have their histories sent north for the correct inspection. This could take a week or more. Meanwhile the poor old buggers were just about penniless and getting desperate, so I'd hassle the Finance Section to crank up a manual payment, which raised more than a few slothful eyebrows and rhetorical observations about the bludgers making people do them favours they didn't deserve.

'Fuck em!' said P37, my workplace neighbour. 'Some of those TPI bastards make more than we do! I just heard that one bloke bought himself a boat and a block of land on Bribie.'

'Gee,' I wanted to say, 'and all he did was get shot at.'

P37 played B-grade district cricket and talked endlessly about a League team named Brothers. Although he was quite young he had a well established beer gut. He went to all the P Section barbecues on Stradbroke Island and told me I should do the same.

'That P1's a pretty good bloke. Likes a good team player. That's the way to get ahead. Hey! You seen the tits on that girl in Personnel? Bazookas, mate! That reminds me. I'm getting married. You'll be doing my job as well as yours.'

Since P37's job seemed to consist of making sure my in-tray was piled four times higher than his, I wasn't particularly bothered by this news.

'Honeymoon? How long will you be gone?'

'Three weeks, but I won't be back here, mate. I've had a promotion.'

'Jeez, next you'll be buying a house.'

He looked very pleased with himself.

'I already have!'

One day, P1 told us we had to take a tour of the Greenslopes Repatriation Hospital to get an idea of the kind of blokes we were looking after.

We went in a mini-bus. Our first stop was the place where they made artificial arms and legs. There was a sign: 'We are the Leonardos of Limbs.' Next we were shown through some of the wards of men who had mortal bewilderment fixed in their eyes, the pages of their history soon to close for good.

Under a shady verandah looking vacantly out onto the hospital lawns sat a man in a vinyl chair.

'Brain dead from too much metho,' said a passing

orderly. He slapped the inmate on the shoulder with friendly indifference. 'Aren't you, mate?'

The old bloke teetered, just retaining his balance. The orderly laughed and strode away. The old bloke laughed and dribbled. He had a crooked back tooth.

Just like Eric.

I didn't know what to do about Eric.

Even though he was working for the Department of Social Security, he was always borrowing money for smack. I didn't mind too much, as I was saving money hand over fist. But there were mutterings at Auchenflower: Eric's popularity was ebbing fast. Some people lent money expecting to get it back.

Another of my duties was to cancel the veterans' pensions when they died. And this was when the absurdity of my 'public service' really hit me. There I was, marking termination forms with symbols the computer would understand, erasing a lifetime of service to flag, to queen, to country, to mere survival in someone else's war. Whatever the case, it had been service real and tangible. And there I was, me who had served no one except myself, who would certainly have run to the wilds of Cape Tribulation had my number come up for conscription to Vietnam, bidding farewell to little pieces of history. Me, who had never created any significant history of my own and was not likely to.

I was sitting at my desk feeling depressed at the likelihood of being doomed to years of transfers and terminations when P1 called me to his office.

'You know, Ian, there's a future for you here. By the end of the year you'll be eligible for permanency. Superannuation, the whole package. There's a vacancy opening up at the end of the month. I could have you acting in the position if you're committed to working here. What do you say?'

He gave me a paternalistic smile of encouragement. When I hesitated his look became puzzled.

'Well?'

I shuffled my sandals on his carpeted floor and looked at him in his neat grey suit and striped tie and I saw what I would become after twenty years of servitude. A claustrophobic panic welled up inside me. I could barely choke out the words.

'I'll think about it.'

He looked mightily displeased.

'Don't think too long. There are other talents around this place.'

But I was already out the door.

I hurried past P3 and the flexitime book, failing to note my precipitate departure at the unusual hour of 10.37 am, and fled for the lifts.

Outside I stumbled through the busy streets. Mute faces flowed along in an ignorant stream, forever trapped by the Cosmic Yawn.

I had to escape. I ran and ran, pushing my way through the crowds. People shouted at my rudeness. They didn't understand. My life was ending before it had begun. There had to be more to my existence than a lifetime in P Section.

Eric moved out of the rat-race. He went to live with Marion in a self-constructed, self-sufficient shanty by a river in the hills behind Maleny. He had promised me he would kick the smack to make things work out. He really sounded like he had his act together.

Unlike me. I found myself lying to P1 about my commitment to the public service and accepting the promotion. The extra money went straight into my bank account on the assumption that one day, I would escape to the spiritually purifying mountains of India.

But I think I knew I was lying to myself as well as to P1. All my talk about being a beggar on the road to self-enlightenment was exactly that – talk. There wasn't a *saddhu*'s bone in my body. So what sort of bones did I have? I had no idea. All I knew was that with Eric up at Maleny, I was lonely as hell.

Until Amy did me an honourable sisterly service.

Hillary, the girl who had worked at Mum's kennels and was now working at Queensland Railways, was a good friend of Amy's. Hillary's twenty-first birthday was approaching, and Amy decided to throw her a party at Auchenflower.

There was much cleaning and tarting up. All the Camelot regulars were coming, even Eric. Marion had given him a wad of cash and instructions to return to Maleny with some second-hand furniture. He arrived in time to help with the decorations. The stereo was blaring and we'd already cracked a flagon. It was going to be a fine party.

Amy handed me a bunch of streamers to hang.

'I want you on your best behaviour tonight.'

'Why?'

She put on a mysterious half-smile.

'You'll find out.'

I hung the streamers and helped Eric string the huge hand-painted HAPPY 21ST HILLARY sign as the stereo roared on. We looked at each other in mild surprise when we discovered that the flagon was nearly empty.

'Ian,' said Amy, with warning in her voice. 'That was meant to last all night.'

'Then we'd better get down to the Regatta and get some more.'

The Regatta billowed cigarette smoke and reeked of stale beer. Everyone was wearing Stubbies and thongs and singlets and lighting up to add to the smoky pall. The bartender was flat out pouring beers without turning the taps off, glass after glass in a continuous stream. We started on ours as we racked up the pool balls.

When Eric rolled up his sleeves to make his shots more comfortable, I saw that his arms were brown and muscled. There was almost no sign of the purple tracks that had once dotted his veins like a map of the road to hell.

'You are kicking!'

Eric gave me a shy smile.

'Told you I would.'

Except he hadn't.

'God!' said Christine the housemother upon our noisy sunset return to Auchenflower. 'You two smell like a brewery.'

Amy ordered us to shower before the guests arrived. I emerged perfumed and presentable in my slightly grubby Levis and an Indian-style white cotton shirt.

'You're not wearing that!' Christine was resplendent in big gold baubles and a florid 1950s-style party dress. Hauling me into her room, she rummaged in a trunk full of dubious costumery and emerged with a pair of black tuxedo trousers, a black satin cummerbund and a knee-length gold-coloured Chinese housecoat heavily embroidered with red dragon and floral patterns. I was wearing this bizarre rig when people started turning up for the festivities.

Julie the vet-to-be had invited her sister Lucy.

'So you're the guy who put the hard word on Julie.'

'Not that it did me any good.'

'You could put the hard word on me . . .'

So I did. We groped and wrestled in my room, the noise of the party – and was it Amy? – hammering at the door.

When we emerged back into the rage, trying to focus on the sea of faces and dancing bodies, I went for a fresh glass of wine. Amy gave me a far from friendly thump on the arm.

'You idiot! You'd better start behaving yourself. She'll be here soon.'

'Who'll be here soon?'

Her answer inspired awe and sudden panic. 'Toni, you fool. For God's sake, get some coffee or something.'

'Toni? She's coming here?'

'Will you stop drinking so much! Yes she's coming

here. The only reason she's late is because she's working.'

'Yeah.' The sour recollection. 'Door duties with Dave and the drummer.'

'Don't you know anything? She's bartending at the National. She broke up with the drummer.'

I made a beeline for the kitchen and plugged the kettle in for coffee. Three spoons full.

'Hello, Ian. Nice to meet you again.'

She was amazingly pretty.

'Wanna dance?'

'Sure.'

We worked a path into the middle of the dance maw and I flung myself about like a flea on acid. We danced until Toni politely pointed out that she was getting kinda sweaty and could use a cool drink.

'No problem!' I rushed off to the fridge for ice and the flagon and when I returned some bastard was trying to move in on Toni. I hoped to Christ the other bloke would go away. He did, because Toni ignored him.

'So, Ian, tell me about yourself.'

What was I to say? That I was a twenty-two year old public servant who'd travelled up and down the Australian eastern seaboard stuffing up every relationship I'd ever had, a never-was writer, a never-was guru. And a liar as well.

'I write poems and songs and things. What about you?'

In the roar I discovered that Toni was from Wisconsin. She'd lived in Spain, London and Northumberland. A few years back she'd sailed with her boyfriend for Perth via

Singapore and taken the trans-Nullarbor train to Melbourne. She had a five-year-old kid named Jimmy.

I was slightly stunned. Toni looked barely twenty.

'Anyway, I hated Melbourne. We stayed just long enough to save some bread and get up to the Daintree. That was beautiful. But I had to rescue my poor pussycat from getting squished by a python and my boyfriend was screwing around on me, so I took Jimmy on the train ride down from Cairns, and here we are.'

'Wow.' I certainly was a conversationalist.

'So, what are you writing at the moment?'

How could I say it? Nothing.

'I'll get something to show you.'

I searched among the debris in my room for the diary I had scribbled in just in case one day someone asked to see what I was writing. I opened to the page where I'd copied down some lines from W.B. Yeats's *The Second Coming*.

They'd do. No, she'd know. I'd be exposed as the full-scale fraud I was.

A black lethargy hit me. My head started reeling and lurching. I sat down on the bed to regain my balance but the spinning got worse. In a matter of seconds, my quest to impress the well-travelled and lovely woman waiting out there for proof of my artistry ended with the artist passing out.

I stepped wincing into the merciless morning light. Amy was making a fierce racket vacuuming the bilge of the night.

She turned off the vacuum and eyed me stonily.

'You were a big hit, I must say.'

'What happened?'

'What do you think happened? You passed out. Some guy tried to crack on to Toni while she was sitting on the couch waiting for you. She was bloody nearly raped before she finally got fed up and called a cab.'

I considered this in silence.

Amy fired up the vacuum and turned away.

'Where's Eric?'

'How should I know?'

I searched the house. I found him in the room once occupied by Marion.

He was flat on the bed. At first I thought he was dead. There was a belt still wrapped around his upper arm. A needle lay on the sheet where it had fallen, a little fleck of blood congealed on the tip.

I examined my fallen friend. He was breathing faintly, unconscious from smack and alcohol.

I shut the door and searched the room until I found the contraband – a ball of heroin that would have cost a lot of money.

Marion's money.

'Shit, Eric. You fucking fool.'

'I think,' Eric said, 'I am in deep shit.'

'Get rid of the smack. Get the money back. Buy the furniture and go back to Maleny.'

Eric shook his head.

'I've used half of it.'

'I'll lend you the balance. Nobody needs to know. Eric, you fucked up once, but if you keep it clean from now on, you'll still be okay.'

I must have sounded like I was making sense. He nodded.

'I'll go to the bank first thing Monday. How much do you need?'

'Two hundred?'

'You spent the lot!'

'Just about.'

'Well, just promise me the money will go on furniture.'

'It will.'

But, of course, it didn't.

Amy called Toni to apologise on my behalf.

'God knows why, Ian, but she's agreed to give you a second chance. Meet her at the pub tomorrow. And don't blow it this time.'

When I got there, Toni was already sitting at a table chatting to a bloke who was standing with his hand against the spare chair. He was obviously hoping to be asked to sit down. The other chair was occupied by a kid who I assumed to be Jimmy. He was pushing a toy car through a lemonade puddle he'd created for the purpose.

I went to the bar and ordered a pot, guzzling it down to settle my guts. The interloper at Toni's table finally got the message and left. My cue.

'Why didn't you rescue me sooner?' There was no accusation, she didn't even wait for an answer. 'This is Jimmy. Jimmy, this is Ian.'

The kid gave me a so-what glance and went back to making wet-wheel tracks. This left me no option but to deliver my apology for the other night.

'Well, I was pretty pissed at you. And when I got home, that creepy guy from the party had followed me and he tried to climb in through my bedroom window.'

'Jeez! What'd you do?'

'Slammed it shut on his knuckles and told him to get the hell out before I called the cops.' Then, the matter apparently forgotten, 'How about a drink? I'll have a Bloody. Three drops of Tabasco and plenty of pepper. Then you can walk me home and I'll show you my house.'

We hitched a ride from Toowong towards the university and crossed the river to West End on the St Lucia ferry. Toni held Jimmy's hand and told me the house's history.

'The whole band used to live at Daventry Street. Before they became such a big hit and they all got girls. Then they wanted places of their own to house their big star egos. When they split up we got the house all to ourselves again.'

'So you were there first?'

'Yep. When we came down from Cairns after that awful railway ride.' She looked at me speculatively. 'Hillary and Amy helped me find it. Didn't you know?'

'No.'

She laughed. 'They've told me all about you.'

Toni's house was desperately in need of paint. The roof was rusty, and the battered wooden front door and sash windows on either side were streaked with weather and neglect.

'No Taj Mahal,' Toni admitted as she searched for her keys. 'But the rent's only thirty bucks a week.'

Jimmy ran inside to find an armload of Lego. He immediately started adding it to a half-constructed castle that was under way on the wooden coffee table in the middle of the small lounge room. This was a cosy room with a couch covered in cotton throw-rugs and blankets, a faded Persian carpet, a stereo, a bookshelf and a brand new television.

Toni went off to fire up the kettle and I did some exploring.

The bookshelf was crammed with works I'd never seen before. Gabriel Garcia Marquez, JP Donleavy, William Gaddis, VS Naipaul, Peter Matthiesen, Cervantes, Jack London, Ernest Hemingway, Hunter S Thompson, Tom Wolfe, Tom Robbins, and a solar system full of sci-fi books that would have put Eric in orbit for weeks.

I moved over to the stereo to check out the offerings there. George Gershwin, Aaron Copeland and Leonard Bernstein's. *West Side Story* mixed with Jerry Jeff Walker's 'It's a Good night for Singin', and Guy Clark's 'Texas Cookin'. The Flying Burrito Brothers and the Ozark Mountain Daredevils. There was a track on one album called 'I'll fix your flat tyre, Merle'.

'So, did you ever find a poem to show me?'

Toni handed me a steaming mug, no doubt aware that she had clobbered me with a question I wasn't ready for. I could sense her warning: don't crap me this time or you are history.

'No. Truth is, I haven't written anything for ages.'

'Not since Lindall with the nut-brown hair.'

I looked at this gorgeous intelligent girl who hardly knew me.

'They've told you everything.'

'Knowledge is power,' she acknowledged cheerfully. 'Say, you want to stay for dinner? I'm a red-hot cook, aren't I, Jimmy?'

'Yesh.'

When I returned to Auchenflower that night, my stomach was mightily satisfied by a sensational veal Parmagiana. My soul was also content because Toni and I had made a date to see a movie together in town.

Eric was missing.

'He said he was going furniture shopping,' said Amy. 'Name a furniture shop that's open on Sunday. Ian, if he's fucking around on Marion . . .'

'He's not. He's . . . I dunno. I hope he's okay.'

There was no point looking for him. In the morning I went to the bank and withdrew the agreed amount plus a hundred more just in case Eric was still on his death-wish. I went to work and waited for his call.

It came via a cop at the Valley police station.

'You know Eric Masters?'

'Yes.'

'He needs someone to guarantee bail.'

Shit.

'How much?'

'Five hundred. You going to go surety?'

'Yes.'

The cop gave me the address.

'What's the charge?'

'Use of narcotics. Possession for sale.'

I flexed off for the day and went to bail him out. He looked hollow. His crooked grin was twisted with guilt.

'What happened?'

'I just wanted one more taste.'

'One more then one more then one bloody more! Fuck, Eric! I haven't got any more money for the furniture. And even if I did, Marion's going to find out now.'

'I know.'

'She'll give you the boot, nothing surer.'

'I know.'

'What are you going to do?'

'What can I do? Cop it.'

'Look, maybe it's not too late. Swear off the smack. Don't touch it ever again. Apologise to Marion, promise to pay her back. Plead guilty. Say you're sorry. Grovel. Start again!'

He gave me a weary shake of the head.

'I'm fucked, Ian. This time I'm fucked.'

Eric moved back to his old room at Auchenflower after Marion summarily kicked him out of Maleny.

'You're lucky she didn't charge you,' I told him.

'Whose side are you on?'

'Yours, Eric. But shit. You ripped off your own girlfriend!'

That silenced him. He looked disgusted – with himself? I couldn't tell.

'What will you do at the court case?'

'Like you said, grovel. Hopefully get off with a fine and a slap on the knuckles.'

'Then what?'

'What else? Find a job and pay the fine off.'

'Then what?'

He slammed a drawer shut and gave me an angry glare.

'Ian, you're starting to give me the shits.'

I stuck to my guns.

'It's just that I've bailed you out before.'

'Oh, pardon me. I must have been mistaken. I thought that's what friends were for.'

'Not any more, it isn't.'

Seven hundred dollars was hardly a slap on the knuckles. Instead of finding a job, Eric sold his car. There was a bit of money left over. We didn't see him for days.

There are times in everyone's life when they make choices that impact on others as much as themselves. I'd ignored Eric's plight once before when I had immersed myself in Simone Simpson. Now I was doing it again.

My relationship with Toni was taking off like one of those new space shuttles. Eric hardly counted.

Not that our first date had been much to write home about. We went to see *Rocky* at a city cinema. Out of consideration for what I perceived to be Toni's liberated status, we went Dutch. Not wishing to push my luck, I kept my hands to myself. After the show, rather than asking what she would like to do, I steered us into a nearby coffee shop and ordered raisin toast and chamomile tea. After Toni had politely consumed her share, I allowed her to travel home alone in a taxi. I can still see her looking at me, astonished, through the back window as the driver pulled away.

'Well, that sounds like fun,' said Amy, when I returned to Auchenflower full of chivalrous self-congratulations. 'I'd better call to make sure she didn't die of boredom on the way home.'

Next time, I went to the National and waited for Toni to finish work. She slipped me a few beers and rolled her eyes good-naturedly at me when the guys from the band took a break and came full of lewd suggestions to the bar for their freebies. I kept my jealousy in check and we went for late night pizza and chianti in the Valley.

'Does it bother you that I have a kid?'

'Why should it? He's a good little bloke. And if I'm going to be spending time with you, well, it would be nice if he liked me, too.'

Toni's lovely face was reflective.

'He's seen a few guys come and go. I think he's reserving his judgement.'

'What about you?'

'Oh, I already know.'

I would have been alarmed at the ambiguity if Toni hadn't put her hand on mine and smiled as she said it. That night, there were two in the taxi.

The next time Eric went missing, he ended up in hospital.

'What's the matter with him?' Toni wanted to know.

'Hepatitis. Again.'

'You should go see him.'

'Why? He'll just want another favour.'

'Ian, he's your friend. You Aussies are always going on about mateship. You have to go see him.'

I didn't refuse, but I didn't say yes, either. Toni showed a genuine flash of anger.

'Well, goddammit, I will!'

And she did. She even asked to see a social worker and helped Eric line up a disability pension to pay the rent at Auchenflower while he recovered. When she came home I copped the cold shoulder. It was bloody frosty. There were times, I had discovered, when apologies just made things worse.

One night after Toni started talking to me again, she told me something important.

'You know how I told you my boyfriend was screwing around on me?'

'And then you came down from Cairns on the train.'

'Yes. Well, he did too, soon afterwards. He kidnapped Jimmy and took him to Melbourne.'

'Oh, Toni.'

'Anyway, I wasn't letting him get away with that, so I went down to Melbourne and kidnapped Jimmy straight back again. We hitch-hiked back here. The whole time, I was terrified he'd catch up with us and there'd be a god-awful scene. I'm still scared he'll come back.'

'You think he will?'

'Yes. Sooner or later. He has to have the last word on everything. And he's a vengeful bastard. He'll come back.'

'Well, what if we go someplace he can't follow?'

'I don't get you.'

'You've been saving to go back to Milwaukee. I'm still saving like buggery. I was thinking we could pool our resources. I could get someone from Deakin University to set us up with some student passes and we could get a discount flight. Maybe go via Europe. You could show me around, then we could go to the States.'

'What about your job?'

I shrugged.

'If I don't get out and see some of the world now, I'll never do it.'

'You'd do that for me?'

'And for me.'

Toni gave me the happiest hug I had ever received.

The news sent Paul off spluttering again.

'What do you mean you're quitting the public service?'

'Exactly that. I've lined up casual work at Lennon's. Plus I'll be driving a delivery van four hours in the morning. Combined, I'll be making much more money.'

'And getting yourself absolutely nowhere in the mean-time. With some girl you've only just met! Chuck everything in, and off you go.'

'Yep.'

'Ian, sometimes I think you must have been damaged at birth. She has a child! You don't know what you're getting yourself into.'

He looked at Mum for support, but all he saw was her warm maternal glow.

'He'll do what he wants, Paul. He always does.'

It was well after midnight. We were smooching on the couch with Jimmy Connors and Bjorn Borg going hammer and tongs in the Wimbledon final when there was a pounding on the door.

It was Eric.

'I fear,' he said, lurching slightly, 'that I've been kicked out of Auchenflower.'

I was surprised. Decisions like that were supposed to happen only through a majority house decision.

'Christine and Julie said I have until rent day to catch up or I'm out.'

Toni and I both knew that he didn't have a cent.

'Well,' Toni said, 'you'll just have to stay here.'

Eric subsided into a chair.

'I don't mind admitting I was hoping you'd say that. I've nowhere else to go. And your cooking is superior.'

'What about me?' I wanted to ask. But Toni must have read my mind.

'You just about live here anyway. Why not make it official? We'll save even more.'

Eric and I moved in simultaneously. But the bitterness of the recent months had not eased.

'So, you're running off again.'

'Why does everyone continually bloody accuse me of running?'

'It's what you do best,' said Eric. 'From Canberra. From Brisbane. From Shute. From Canberra again. From Geelong. Need I go on?'

'This is different.'

'Why?'

'Because I'm going towards something. I have no idea what, but it's not from, it's to. At least you might admit I'm showing some guts.'

'Brave Ian! Off into the unknown with woman and child in tow.'

'At least I won't go squirting her money up my veins.'

Eric looked like he wanted to deck me. Maybe he only restrained himself because this time, unlike the days when we were kids, I would have hurt him. He satisfied himself with a bit of stern advice.

'You can say what you like. But when I needed help, in the crunch it was Toni who came through for me, not you. She's the one who'll be leaving me with a roof over my head. So just don't abandon her as soon as the going gets tough. Okay, I fucked things up with Marion. That's my responsibility. Just make sure you live up to yours.'

By the time he had finished, his anger had subsided completely.

'You'll do that, won't you?'

'Yes, Eric. I will.'

Somewhere in my collection of memorabilia there is a photo of Eric at our farewell party.

His eyes are red from the flash and too much grog, but looking closely I can see hints of sadness and defiance. Perhaps he realised that it was the end of our long road together.

Toni and I did not return to Australia for three years. While we were gone, Eric did a stretch in Boggo Road gaol and another in Goulburn gaol. He suffered recurring bouts of hepatitis. Eventually he was allowed legal access to methadone, and he was still on it years later.

Eric's look at the camera foretells it all. That crooked smile so defiant and guilty all at once. The careless shrug of those narrow shoulders that seemed to say, as matter-of-fact as ever, *'C'est la guerre'*.

He was right. Life is war. Battles and skirmishes against the mortal enemy, the Cosmic Yawn.

How you beat the yawn is up to you. Taste, test, win, lose, rise triumphant, fall defeated. Just do it your way, and don't drag anyone else down with you. And, whatever you do, don't give up.

Eric hasn't. He told me so, just the other day.

Also by Wakefield Press

Rage of Angels
Expatriate Tales

Barry Westburg

Rage of Angels juxtaposes weirdly comic scenes from the several lives of Rick Richards, expatriate Yank, and other maimed menfolk and wounded women who have become lost in space, unzipped in time. Sometimes real life – with its cornshuckings, rusted Mustangs, haunted Rhineland castles, surfing sergeants, violated villas, Asian chicken shops, piping shrikes, IVF clinics and water babies – can dissolve into a cartoon Western or a road movie. And almost always does.

'Barry Westburg's short stories are fantasies of another order – American Midwestern noir, Australian suburban dreaming, hilarious memoirs, enigmatic fables, literary theory games and surreal satire.'　　　　Michael Sharkey, *Australian*

ISBN 1 86254 448 4　　RRP $19.95

Also by Wakefield Press

In Elizabeth
A frontier novel

Stewart Henderson

Forget those undulating English names – the Downs, the Vale, the Grove: Elizabeth was a frontier town, flat, dry, harsh and lawless.

Danny Russell, precocious child of Scottish emigrants, is a born survivor. He soon goes native in working-class Elizabeth, South Australia's new model city. In the dusty streets and playgrounds of Elizabeth, Danny and his friends learn to live by their wits. Theirs is a world of stolen pleasures and elemental violence, of endless variations on the battle between Good and Evil, though to them it was a more straightforward question of whether to Kill or Be Killed.

In this startling first novel, Stewart Henderson casts a bold and ironic eye over the frustrations and fantasies of growing up on the urban frontier.

ISBN 1 86254 412 3   RRP $17.95

Also by Wakefield Press

Eye of the White Hawk

Stories by Bary Dowling

In *Eye of the White Hawk* Bary Dowling tells stories rich in
their evocation of a world close to nature. Set in the city, or
rural Australia, or the bush, these are stories of interior lives,
and of transformations achieved through effort, seeking and
discovery, a process that never stops.

'A special virtuosity that brings us back with a jolt to believe
the centre of the world is not urban, or suburban, but in the
silences of our own landscape. Dowling strikes gold.'

Thomas Shapcott

ISBN 1 86254 421 2   RRP $17.95

Also by Wakefield Press

the skinscape voyeur

Neil Paech

Here are love poems from Hindley Street, North Terrace, the Mall, Rundle Street, Gouger Street, the Central Market, Chinatown, North Adelaide and Willunga. This collection follows the success of Neil Paech's *K is for Keeper, A is for TV* and *The Bitumen Rhino*.

ISBN 1 86254 406 9   RRP $14.95

Wakefield Press has been publishing good Australian books
for over fifty years. For a catalogue of current and
forthcoming titles, or to add your name to our mailing list,
send your name and address to

Wakefield Press, Box 2266, Kent Town, South Australia 5071.

TELEPHONE (08) 8362 8800   FAX (08) 8362 7592
WEB www.wakefieldpress.com.au

Wakefield Press thanks Wirra Wirra Vineyards and
Arts South Australia for their continued support.